True Diamond

By

Jennifer Luckett

Dedication: I dedicate this novel to one of the coolest young chicks to enter the literary game. Author MiAmor, 'Destiny Smith' I miss you dearly 'D'. Can't believe that you're never coming back again. There's a saying that says, The good die young. And, I believe every word of it. Sometimes it's crazy when I have to accept people into the Facebook group that we administered together, Urban Fiction Lovers. I'm so used to you handling that part for me. (smile) I'll miss your texts and your east coast accent when you would hit me up about the industry asking for my opinion on something. Sleep in paradise, princess.☺

One Thang After Another

Sayveon

Ah, damn! Too much shit was jumping off at the same time, and it was taking me off my square. Just when I thought I was finally 'bout to get some peace, some mo' bullshit went down. If my mom had of been on the up and up 'bout who my real pops was, I wouldn't have been balls deep inside Carmen. I didn't use a rubber. Now she's claiming she's preggos by me. On the real, that situation right there had me feeling so low I could hardly hold my head up. What set it off was when she said she was keeping it. The chick was trippin'.

I didn't have a problem taking care of my kid but not one by my blood. Hell nah. Wasn't happenin'. Furthermore, I didn't even want mothafuckas in the street to even hear 'bout nothing like that 'bout me. I'd have mofos laughing behind my back at that right there. I had a boss image to uphold. Plus, I didn't want all that talk getting back to Pops. It was no way in the world I'd let that right there go down. I'd blow the broad off the map before I let it happen. I wouldn't think twice 'bout wettin' her up. It was nothin'.

I lifted my body from my bed and paced back and forth in my bedroom, thinking. I then sauntered to the back door and opened it. A cool breeze from the October weather hit as soon as my foot touched the ground. I bounced down in one of the wood chairs with my cell pressed against my ear; I was trying to digest what she had said.

"Wait a minute. Hol' up. You say you having this li'l mothafucka?" I asked to be sho' my ears weren't playing games on me.

"Yes, I'm going to have it," she replied with attitude.

"You got to be losing yo' mothafuckin' mind." I cocked my head to the side in disbelief.

"I'm sane, and I said I'm keeping it. Clean the wax out of your ears, and maybe we can get a clear understanding," she said, shit talking.

"Man, get the fuck out of here wit' that shit. We kinfolk, and if I had of known that Big Al was my real daddy, I wouldna never touched you." I wanted to resolve the matter. "Look, check this out. We both fucked up, and there's only one way to fix this and make it good. You need to get rid of it. I'll pay fo' everythang," I tried to convince her.

"You're a player, and you just don't want the responsibility of having to take care of another baby."

"It ain't got nothing to do with me being a playa, so you can get off of that. You kno' this ain't cool. That li'l mofo gon' be fucked up; we're too closely related." I rubbed my hand down my sideburn, shaking my head and dreading the day I fucked her.

I heard her smack her lips. "Sayveon, stop it. You wanted to holler the minute you laid eyes on me. Now you're trying to act like it's my entire fault."

I raised the corner of my lip and frowned. "Shawdy, you came in the room where I was begging fo' me to put some wood in you. You were jockin' my swag. I wasn't on you like that. And right now, I ain't gon' go back and forth on who wanted who. Just handle what you got to handle, and we straight."

There was a brief silence on the phone. And, I was tired of dealing with her and her *Young and The Restless* drama. It felt like everything around me was falling and when I bounced back, something else was waiting to try to knock me down. But, I was G from the feet up. I couldn't be fazed.

My thoughts were broken when she spoke. "I will call the clinic now and see how much it is to have this done, but maybe this will teach you a lesson about sticking your penis here, there, and everywhere. I'll call you back."

About five minutes went by when Carmen's name popped up on my cell. I answered. "I need you to take me to the clinic in the morning. I've scheduled an appointment. The first visit is for the consultation, and the second one is for the procedure to be done," she said, giving me relief.

I sighed a long hard sigh. "Aight, good."

"I need you to come pick me up at nine o' clock in the morning. I'm going to need four hundred and fifty dollars too."

"Aight, I got you covered."

"I'll see you in the morning," she said, dryly like she still wasn't sure 'bout her decision.

"Later."

I hung up with her, and my mind went from that situation to my daughter, Layla. Sparkle had been on some foul shit and wouldn't answer my calls or text messages when I tried to reach out to her to see the baby. Even though I had been spending time with Janay, it didn't make up for me missing my other seed. Not only did I miss my babygirl, but I missed Sparkle too. I knew thangs were too far gone for me to get back what me and Sparkle once shared. So, I chalked that up and moved on. With the family that I once had on my mental, I walked back inside the crib and heard the doorbell ring. I ambled to the front and peeped through one of the blinds. I thought my eyes were trippin'. It was my BM, Sparkle.

Breaking The News

Sparkle

There I stood at Sayveon's front door, full of baby, thinking, *I hope one of his dirty tricks ain't in here 'cause today is not the day, and tomorrow ain't looking much better.* On the way over, I considered dialing his digits instead of showing up, but hell nah, I needed to see his trifling ass face to face. I wanted to at least talk this thing out like two adults. I had fucked up bad by being pregnant by his doggish, self-centered ass. I felt about as stupid as Sayveon looked when he opened the door.

"What you want?" he asked in a dry tone, mugging me up and down only wearing black boxers and a pair of white ankle socks. Being shirtless exposed his smooth and muscular chest, washboard stomach, and six-pack. I quickly looked away from his body. I felt like I was cheating on my man. Ontavious truly loved me and I would never betray him in any kind of way. He was everything that I had asked God for, and I loved him and didn't want to lust over any other man.

I folded my arms across my chest. "I need to talk to you about something."

"C'mon in then," he responded. He made his way into the living room area a few feet away and plopped down into his recliner. I trailed behind and bopped down on the sofa directly in front of him, checking out his crib.

The plush coffee-brown leather sofa faced the door, and everything was nice and neat with brand-new furniture. The living room area had classic designs including a coffered ceiling and ocular windows. The double adjoined French doors inlaid with glass looked gorgeous. The beautiful addition opened from the middle and created a nice outside view. I twisted my neck and noticed the fireplace. It had a traditional mantle that nicely sat on a dark stained Brazilian cherry hardwood floor. Normally, it was my job to decorate the inside of the home, but he was most certainly maintaining without me. I once thought that he couldn't live without me, but the way the house was decorated showed me otherwise.

At times, I missed Sayveon. Although we had a long history together, I knew that he couldn't be trusted. I didn't trust him as far as I could throw him, which wouldn't be far. Furthermore, I was devoted to Ontavious. He made me happier than I had been in a long time. I knew he was the best choice for me, yet a piece of my heart would always love Sayveon. Sayveon was my first boyfriend, my first kiss, and my first love. Most importantly, we shared a special bond between us, Layla.

He silently sat running his eyes over my frame. I had no idea whether he wanted to knock the shit out of me or what. The last time we saw one another was when I saw him with his date who turned out to be his sister. That's the night I was in the truck with Ontavious. I was in a weird position at his crib wondering if he'd get up and rap my ass, or if he was plotting to body me.

"The gate's entrance was wide open. Normally, it's locked, and I used to have to use my remote or either enter the code for it to open," I said to break the ice.

"They say it's broken, but it's supposed to get fixed by the end of the week." Switching topics he asked, "Where's the baby?"

"She's with my auntie. I came over here to tell you that I'm pregnant," I blurted out waiting for his response.

He bucked his eyes and looked at me like I was crazy. "You need to tell this to whoever you fuckin'."

"Boy, get yo' life. I guess you think you talking to one of yo' bird ass tricks out in the streets. Its yo' baby," I told his simple minded, cocky ass.

"Go holla at ole' boy you was in the truck wit' and tell him he 'bout to have a shawty on the way," he clowned.

I put up my pointer finger. "Hold up. Don't give me no jazz. 'Cause you were having just as much fun as I was. You had that Carmen trick in yo' whip. Don't try to call me out like you were out doing right and... This--- ain't--- his--- baby," I slowly clarified.

He rose up in the recliner, stared at the floor for a brief moment, and his eyes landed on me again. "I'll get a blood test done 'cause when I scoped you out wit' my own two eyes, I knew it was a wrap fo' us. It made me wonder what other niggas you had been creepin' wit' behind my back."

I knew he was trying to tongue slap me by throwing an insult about taking a DNA, but I didn't bite the bait. I didn't want to add alcohol to the burning fire, and I didn't go there with the intention of arguing. I wanted to talk to him and hold an adult conversation about the pregnancy. He was already flipping the conversation on me insinuating that I had been dirty macking on him behind his back. In reality, his unfaithfulness is what led me into Ontavious' arms. At that point, I could feel the situation forming into a dispute, and the tension was slowly rising like dough.

"You fucked him yet?" he boldly asked.

"Did you fuck Carmen?" I shot back.

"Answer me, and don't ask a question wit' a question," he bossed.

"Who I'm fucking is no longer your business or concern. I'm sure you fucked Carmen. Don't make me remind you that she's your sister. Now, that's some nasty shit," I tooted my lip up and rolled my eyes, in disgust.

"Me and her kicked it only that one night but I ain't never piped her."

Sayveon held a straight face, but I couldn't ever believe much that rolled off his tongue. He lied more than a politician.

"Sayveon, lying is just another part of your life. You wouldn't be able to get through the day being honest," I hurled. I decided to get ready to go before the confusion blew up and got out of hand.

"I'm being straight up. Since I'm keepin' it real wit' you, I need you to be honest wit' me. You got my daughter 'round another nigga, don't you?" he asked flipping the topic once again.

"Layla is being well taken care of. Whoever I choose to have around my daughter will be someone who I can trust," I admitted. At the end of the day, Layla was still his daughter, but whether I had another man around her really wasn't his business. Yet in still, I wanted him to know that she was safe, and I would never put my child in harm's way. "You shouldn't be mad, due to the fact that you had her around that Nakia chick. Is she still claiming to be pregnant by you?"

"I haven't heard from her lately."

It was funny how he had so many thirsty chicks around him while we were together. I'm sure they were still sweating him, but I kinda thought it was worse when we were together. His maggots felt that I was their competition, and I knew that the bitches didn't like me. I could tell that Sayveon hadn't changed his doggish ways because he was still trying to lie his way out of anything that I asked him. His track record was proof that he'd lie and hump anything that walked.

"Wow! She's prob'ly laid up with the next nigga. You've shitted on me so many times until I don't give a damn. You never learned from your mistakes you just kept right on doing whatever you wanted to. You stepped all over my heart, and I loved you. These hoes out here only love you while your pockets on swollen, but you can't see that." I shrugged my shoulders. He simply--- didn't get it.

"Stop trippin'. I kno' all broads want is to play me out of my pockets, I'm game tight. That's why I chose you as 'wifey.' You had been down wit' me before I had bank, popped tags, and splurged in the streets. I owed you that out of the respect that you had been down wit' me from jump. That's why I made sure you had the best of er' thang. You had thousand dollar minks, diamond rings, a new whip, and you had my heart. Ask any hoe out here in the streets if I ever paid their bills or bought 'em fly whips fresh off the lot. I only did that shit wit' you." He folded his arms across his chest and placed one leg over the arm of the chair.

"You're right," I admitted. "I'll give props where they are due. You took excellent care of me, and I am very appreciative. Yet in still, I don't want to keep having altercations with your chickens on the side. Not only that, I don't wanna be walking 'round here with my pussy itching or coochie bumps. You be doin' the most wit' these ratchet bitches."

"I ain't ever given you nothing." It seemed that he was trying to justify sleeping around on me in the past.

"Well, if you raw dogged females, you gambled with both of our lives. Damn, do I need to have a sex education class with you?"

"You can *give* me some sex. That's what you can do." He gave me direct eye contact when he said it.

I side eyed him. "You better use your five finger discount."

His cell phone began to ring, breaking up the conversation, and was I ever glad. I wouldn't have let him touch me with a ten foot pole. He grabbed the phone from inside his front jeans pocket, looked to see who was calling, and answered. "Wassup, Pops?" After that, he kept saying, Uh-huh and okay. "I'll see you 'round two o'clock," he told Pops before hanging up.

"I need to make a run in a li'l bit. Pops needs me to come over." He placed the phone on his lap.

I flicked my wrist and looked at my watch. It was already thirty minutes after one o'clock. "I guess I will shove off and let you go on."

"Before you leave I need to give you something for my baby. Hol' up." He raced off, and I heard the sound of his footsteps racing up the stairs. I crept over to the chair where he left his phone behind. I grabbed the device and navigated to the text and voicemail icon. I pressed okay. I strolled down to text and multimedia and browsed through his inbox. My mouth dropped, my body wouldn't move, and I stared at the message from Carmen wide-eyed. I froze and could hardly breathe. The shock began to melt away and everything slowly returned. I let out a long sigh and shut my mouth quickly. I gulped. I released the phone from my grip and dropped it back on the chair. I felt light headed and disoriented. I took a deep breath, trying to block out the memory.

I heard his feet tapping back down the wooden staircase. He showed up and passed some money insisting, "Take this and do something wit' Layla."

I opened my hand and accepted the bills. I stood there fidgeting from nervousness and finally pushed the money down into my bra. "Thanks." I swirled around toward the door and opened it. Who I saw pulling up had me madder than a mofo. As usual, this nigga was 'bout to be in a shit storm.

Unforeseen Bullshit

Sayveon

When Sparkle opened the door, Ginger rolled down the street, whipped into the driveway, and hopped out of her metallic silver new-modeled Acura RL. Ginger's soft pink baby-tee clung to her. Her dark blue skinny jeans gripped her phatty like two hands.

She bounced up to the front door blowing a pink globe of bubblegum. "Excuse me, but am I interrupting something," she sarcastically asked and giggled. Her blue eyes glanced back and forth from me to Sparkle.

I ignored her comment. "Fall the fuck back, Ginger. Don't come to my crib and boss up like you regulating shit over here," I snapped.

"I'm not trying to rule you or your home. I only asked a simple question. Gosh," she whined and twirled a long strand of her blonde hair.

"I'm leaving," Sparkle groaned. "You need to put yo' trick in check. I don't have time for this silly shit right here. This is pitiful how she's coming to your crib being disrespectful." Sparkle brushed right past Ginger.

Ginger pointed her finger at Sparkle, and I knew there were 'bout to be some problems. "Don't you dare touch me, you whore. Don't you make me kick your ass, and you better stay away from my man."

I pushed Ginger. "Back the fuck up, and stop trippin'. Don't disrespect my baby mama and she ain't here to beef. Gon' head and get on down wit' the bullshit." I could smell liquor on her breath. It had to have her gassed up 'cause she wasn't stupid enough to test my gangsta. I raised my hand and bitch slapped her because her tongue had gotten too slick. I grabbed her by the throat and slung her into the front door. She held her face like she couldn't believe that I had hit her.

I heard Sparkle crank her ride up. I turned around and saw her behind the wheel of her automobile. She tooted her horn two times to get my attention. She couldn't leave because Ginger had her blocked in. "Tell that bobble head bitch to come move this piece of shit so I can go. I don't have time for this bullshit. I need to go home to my daughter," Sparkle screamed out of the window.

"Why---did---you ---hit---me?" Ginger asked, and wiped away the tears that dripped from the corner of her eyes. She stood there crying like a baby and all of a sudden, she spit and it ended up on my eyelid, and then she raised her knee and kneed me in the nuts.

I leaned over holding my dick and balls. I took a few deep breaths before I slammed her to the ground and throwed hands on her, bangin' her in the face. I rose up, drug her through the grass, and left her in the middle of the yard. It was just her luck, the water shot from the sprinkler system. Water sprayed all over the grass and Ginger balled up in a fetal position with her arms covering her head. "Turn the water off," she screamed. I jerked her up by the arm and shoved her towards her car.

"Go move yo' car out of my baby mama's way so she can get out. You can mash out right behind her, too," I thundered. "Go get my shit and bring it to me before you go. I told you to fall back, but you want to act hardheaded."

She swirled and faced me. She was soakin' wet, hair matted to her face, and her clothes dripped raindrops of water. "I'm not going to fall back on this ground and hurt myself," the dummy said.

She walked to her ride and told Sparkle, "I bet you fucked him while you were over here, huh?"

Sparkle put up her hand. "Trick, swerve."

"What the hell does that mean?" Ginger asked her looking confused.

"That means get the hell on before I hit yo' ass in the mouth and have you out here leaking. You'sa dense one," Sparkle insulted shakin' her head from side to side.

Ginger lifted her foot and kicked one of the front tires of Sparkle's SUV. I knew right then that shit was 'bout to get worse, and it did.

She Gon' Learn Today

Sparkle

See, when white chicks start getting a piece of black dick it fucks up their whole understanding. I had no intentions of coming to Sayveon's crib for the extra. I only wanted to see how he felt about my pregnancy. I mean, we were 'bout to have another baby together, and that was a serious issue for me. I didn't want to raise another child alone. To be honest, the thought of that had me scared.

I wasn't sure how Ontavious would take the news once I admitted it to him. I was already angry and frustrated from my own personal problems, and here this crazy chick comes with some more stress to add to it. I had taken all I was going to take off her and when she kicked my ride, I knew I had to give her exactly what she was asking for. I was trying to be a nice law abiding citizen, but the blue-eyed devil wouldn't let that happen.

I hopped out, grabbed the blonde skank by her hair, yanked it firmly, and tried to yank it out from the root. I slung her into the hood of my ride and banged the back of her head down on it, repeatedly. If it weren't for Sayveon tugging me away, I would have still been all over that ass like a bad rash. That gave her the perfect opportunity to retaliate. She spun in the air, one of her feet kicked me full strength in the chin, and I thought the trick had broken my jawbone. Both of her feet landed on the ground. She had put another one of her martial arts moves on me.

She squinted her eyes and raised an eyebrow. I could feel the malice come through the gaze. The heifer could have set fires with the power of her wicked eyes. I rubbed the side of my face and my mouth dropped. I was in agony from the blow. I felt a warm liquid flowing down my chin and when it dropped on my brown halter-top dress, I realized that it was strawberry- red blood. I wiped my mouth with the back of my hand. "I'm 'bout to beat you so bad yo' soul gon' hurt," I threatened.

I snatched my arm away from Sayveon and yelled, "Get the fuck away from me, dog."

"Leave this shit alone. You kno' you can't be out here tryna act like this, and you're pregnant," he said.

I thought about the pregnancy and Layla and I shouldn't have been acting a plum fool, but I couldn't let that tramp slide. I turned to try to get in my ride and find something to strike her with. That's when I instantly felt a blow strike me in the back of the head. My head was throbbing, and I had to defend myself at that point. Ginger had caught me off guard and hit me again. That's when Sayveon bitch slapped her a few times. I leaped over, reached through the window, and pressed the button to pop my trunk. I sprinted to the back of my ride and grabbed a weapon. I got all up in her personal space and clocked her with the lug wrench. It popped her left eye and left her dazed. She stumbled backwards from that power blow.

"How dare you," she said as her lips trembled. A few drops of blood oozed down from the open gash over her brow, but I wasn't done beating her down. I charged into her, knocked her onto the slippery grass, and pummeled her. I was mounted on top of her puttin' in work. Bop! Bop! Bop! I busted her in her shit and refused to let up. Even the cold water splashing in my face from the sprinkler system didn't bother me. I had one thing on my mind, *whoopin' that ass til she was black and blue.* I would've still been goin' upside her head if Sayveon hadn't saved her. That's when I looked down and noticed that my titties had popped out of my halter dress and were hanging like two round cantaloupes.

"Ginger, get up and go get what you owe me, and then you can take off," he roared. She slowly lifted her body and struggled to get to her ride. Her hair was all over her head and looked like she'd been electrocuted. I stood there panting and putting my breast back inside my clothing. He was on her trail. She slid behind the steering wheel and started her engine, rolled her window down, reached under the passenger seat, upped a brown bag, and shoved it to him.

I grabbed the lug wrench, dashed over to her car, raised the iron up, and hammered her driver's side window. Crushed glass toppled down on her seat and all over her. She put her car in reverse and started backing out of the driveway. Sayveon blocked a few of my blows. "Stop, Sparkle," he ordered and dropped the bag to the ground in order to pin my arms down to my side. I stood there huffing and puffing almost out of breath. Ginger backed out of the driveway and burned rubber down the street.

I yanked away from Sayveon's grasp and strutted to my ride. My clothes were wringing wet along with my hair, and that shit had me boiling water hot. "I'm so glad I'm done with you wit' yo' dirty ass. You ain't shit, and I hate the day I laid eyes on you, bastard," I let out before getting inside my whip and mashing out. Leaving that clown was the best thing I could have ever done.

I drove home on Interstate 55 in a deep thought. I glanced out of the side window at the large pine trees before focusing my attention back on the highway. I began thinking about my past with my child's father. I had come to learn that love means giving someone the chance to hurt you but trusting that they won't. When I completely trusted someone, without any doubt, I'd automatically get one of two results. I'd find either a friend for life or a lesson for life. In the end, the outcome was always positive.

I had accepted that Sayveon didn't care about me. I weeded him out of my life and made room for those that did. When I continued to give myself to someone who didn't respect me, I had surrendered pieces of my soul that I could never get back. I had acknowledged the fact that he didn't love me the way that I had loved him. Letting go of him was much easier than holding on. I thought it was hard to walk away until I actually did it. Ooh, was I ever glad I had kicked him to the curb.

Back and Better Than Before

Stephanie

My son's father, James, and I had been together for what seemed like eternity. Both of my kids were grown and in college at the University of Southern Mississippi. I hadn't been the best mom over the years, but I had made up my mind that I'd do better. I'm not perfect. Nobody is, and I didn't claim to be. In fact, I'm far from it, but at least I am trying.

I'm a thirty-eight year old top notch chick, or let me rephrase that... I'm a bad broad and proud of it. I'm standing 5'7 with a peanut-butter brown complexion and a body so fly that when I walk I can stop a heartbeat. I had gotten my body back tight with my nice sized c-cup breasts, flat tummy, and sexy curves. I ran into some issues in my life including drug abuse with heroin, but it was only a setback for a major comeback. I'm definitely back and looking better than ever. When dudes checked out my figure and wanted to holla, I would creep on James but he didn't kno' it. I was always told that what's done in the dark will always come to the light. My attitude has always been that if a fish kept its mouth closed, it would never be caught. That was my motto and exactly what I lived by. Some may say that I think I'm the shit now that I'm out the streets. Naw, I'm just secure and very confident, and the confidence developed once I stopped abusing my body.

I had made up my mind that I was done with the drugs and sticking myself like I was a pin cushion. My life had been wild, and I had made some terrible choices and left my sister Sparkle to take care of my boys while I was in the streets. Jason is now twenty-two, and Jacob is twenty years old. They are my everything, and I love them both to death.

I loved James also. He was a good father now and very concerned about our boys getting a good education. He made sure he bought both of them a car. Nothing too fancy or expensive, but they had transportation.

James was able to provide for us because of his job at Nissan. He also decided to further his education so he attended Hinds Community College at night. He studied Petroleum Engineering Technology. I was happy that he was off drugs too and trying to better himself, but he had become boring. We never went out because he was either tired, working, or in class. Not saying I'm ungrateful, but I needed to spend quality time with him. He didn't ask me to clock in on nobody's clock, so I was very grateful for that. He kept money in my pocket and made sure I was financially okay. We had recently moved out of his mama's house and into an apartment in Ridgeland, Mississippi and I liked it a lot. 'Cause living with his nosey mama while she meddled in our business almost drove me nuts.

Speaking of going nuts... I had been home all day watching TV in the family room, bored and lonely as hell. I needed to get out. I had a thought to call Sparkle and see if I could get her out of the house. I scooted to the edge of the sofa where I had laid my cell and dialed up her number.

"What's up, chick?!!" I screamed in her ear the minute I heard her voice.

"What it do, sis?" she asked and let out a giggle. I must have uplifted her spirits because she answered dryly at first.

"Chile, you need to get out of the house. Let's go to the casino and chill later on today," I suggested. I began to bite on my fingernails waiting for her to answer.

"That's cool. Come get me and let's go to Silverstar in Philadelphia. That one is closer to me and that way you can swoop me up."

"Okay. That's wassup. I'll see you in a couple of hours. I'll pick you up around four o'clock. I need to hop in the shower and get jazzy and then I'm on my way."

"See you then. That'll be good 'cause I need to go home and schedule a doctor's appointment and handle some other stuff."

I grinned. "Go 'head and handle your business." I changed the subject. "You kno' they got those good drinks and food up there."

"I hear yo' crazy butt. Talk to you later, and I love you," she told me.

"I love you too, girlie."

I hung up, disconnecting the call. I was more than excited to hang out with Sparkle. Hopefully, we could catch up and mend our broken relationship that had been torn apart by my former heroin addiction.

Some Shit In The Game

Sayveon

Sparkle waited for Ginger to push on, left out of the driveway, and never looked back. I could tell that she was fed up wit' me and my bitches from what she had just said to me. I felt guilty, and I knew that she prob'ly would never show up again or plan to be wit' me after all of that shit went down.

I turned and walked back into my crib. I had almost forgotten that I had to go to Pops and see what was up wit' him. I had to leave, so I locked up the house wit' the large brown bag in my hand. I let the garage door up, went on to my Benz, and hopped in.

I had put my whip in reverse and backed out into the street. My neighbor, Jack, came racing from across the street waving me down. I mashed on brakes and waited for him to cross. "Hey, I was checking my mailbox a few days ago and a black guy was walking down the street. I've never seen him before, but he asked me if a guy named, Sayveon Travis lived over there," he said with his southern tone and pointed at my crib.

"Did he say what he wanted to kno' that fo'?" I questioned, confused.

"He said that he's supposed to be doing some painting for you," Jack reported and scratched the top of his head. He shrugged. "Beats me."

I shrugged too. "I don't kno' who he could've been 'cause I haven't asked anybody to do any painting 'round my crib. And who the hell let him in? If he don't have a remote to the gate then he ain't supposed to be up in here."

"I saw him jump the gate when he got up there." He redirected his pointer finger towards the front entrance where the tall gate was. "I said I was going to ask you 'bout the son-of-a- bitch before I called the cops if I see him back 'round here again."

I nodded my head up and down in agreement. "That's wassup. Good lookin' out."

"No problem." He swirled around and headed back toward his house.

I pushed on down the street knowing my life was in danger. I puzzled my brain tryna figure out if I had any enemies that wanted me dead. I had the altercation with ole' boy who shot me, but I hadn't retaliated, yet. I already had my shit put on fire and blazed up a while back so I had to watch my back. I couldn't worry with all of that at the time. I had too much other shit on my mental, and once I went to see what was up with Pops, I'd try to figure the rest of the bullshit out.

I whipped in Pops' driveway, leaped out my whip, and walked up to his front door. I knocked three times and rang the doorbell. "Who is it?" Pops called out from behind the door.

"It's Sayveon, Pops," I said.

Pops gradually opened the door wit' a cigar stuck between his thumb and index finger. He motioned for me to come in and coughed a few times. Dude was forever coughing, but he wouldn't kill the smokin'. He led me to the outside patio where he was sitting and smoking like a chimney. I took a seat at the small wooden table and placed the bag on top of it.

He removed his cap. He ran his fingers through his stringy silver hair that was once silky and then rubbed the back of his neck. His hands dropped in his lap, and he clenched his fists. From his movement, I knew something was wrong.

He leaned over on the table holding the cigar over the ashtray and used his thumb to flick the ashes. "I'm going to need you and Rich to do some detective work. I'm sending you both down to Miami to check up on some shit. I have a big suspicion, and I need you two to deal with it for me," he insisted.

"What's on yo' mind? Let me kno' the deal." I knew that whatever it was, it was some real shit. Pops was looking stressed as hell.

"Jackie just told me today that she's two months pregnant."

I smiled. "Well, you should be happy." I leaned toward him and playfully punched him on the arm. "You still got it, old man."

Instead of returning a smile, he frowned and dropped his head. "No, son. I had a vasectomy after our youngest daughter was born. I have never told her that I even had the procedure done. I felt that I was getting too old to keep bringing babies in the world."

I knew right then what he was saying without really telling me. "That means the baby ain't yours."

"Right. She's in Florida now supposedly visiting her mother. I'm going to give you all the vital information that you need. I want you and Rich to find out what is going on down there with her. I need to know. She's fucking someone down there, and I know it. My gut feeling is telling me so."

"What you want us to do if we see the dude she's fucking?"

"Handle him, and I'll handle her," he said. He tightly pressed his lips together and looked downward before bangin' his fist on the table. "That whore is in for a rude awakening."

"It'll be aight..." I cut the conversation short when I felt a shock wave and heard a loud, *BOOM!* A loud massive noise went off shaking Pops' crib and shattering a few windows. I hopped up from my seat and took off up front to see that the hell was going on. I noticed that a few picture frames had fallen off the walls and were lying on the floor. I made it to a window and damn near died from what I witnessed. A thick cloud of smoke filled the street and a huge fireball of flames had erupted from my car.

I barged through the door. There was a real strong odor, a pungent smell of gunpowder outside along with a circle of neighbors gathered into the street, gawking at my ride. Now I knew fo' a fact that somebody wanted me murked, but I didn't know who.

A Night Full Of Surprises

Stephanie

At four o' clock on the dot, I was pushing through Auntie Ruby's drive. I glanced out of the window after killing my motor staring at the beauty of the country life. In the distance, there was a big lake. A family of bald eagles ruled the skies and patrolled the body of water. To the right of the lake was a huge red barn surrounded by the maple trees. They were full of every shade of yellow and red leaves due to the fall weather. Watching the stocky cows and horses eat and the seasons change had to be peaceful. The atmosphere was quiet. There were no police and ambulance sirens and no noisy neighbors having parties.

Beside the house, there was a well. When I was younger, I can recall drinking from it. The water had a pleasant hint of taste. A chemical analysis suggested that it is perhaps the healthiest water that Auntie would ever drink. She used to drink one cup of coffee a day and the rest was water, but she never complained.

"Are you goin' to get yo' behind out of the car, or you gon' stay in there?" I heard a voice holler. I quickly snatched my head toward the front door. Aunt Ruby had stuck her head out, smiling.

I opened the door of my new-modeled Ford Fusion and planted my six-inch red spiked heels on the ground. The fresh air hit my nostrils after standing. I closed the car door behind me and sashayed up to the house. I was geared in a hip-hugging cranberry-red tube dress. "You lookin' sharp," Auntie complimented.

"Thank you. I did my best." I stepped inside where the baby was in a baby swing in the family room area swinging back and forth. I embraced Aunt Ruby. She gave me a wet kiss on the jaw. It was funny how the elders, especially in the country, loved to smack a person's jaw with their lips. That was a sign of nothing but love. I moved over to the baby and grabbed her out of the swing. "Hey, Auntie Steph's precious niece," I greeted. She was so adorable and cute, and I have to mention chubby. I let out a loud laugh when she smiled at me. Her plump jaws felt so soft against my face when I kissed her.

"Sit down and get comfortable," Auntie said and patted on the cushion of the couch right beside her.

I flopped down holding the baby. "Oooh. Somebody has pooped and made a mess," I said and got tickled at my remark. Layla had a bowel movement and began to cry. "Hold on. I'll change you, precious. You ain't got to cry," I spoke in baby talk. My aunt left out of the room and brought back a diaper, baby wipes, and baby powder. I laid her on her back and started changing her. "It's been so long since I've changed a diaper."

"You better not get that stuff on you, or you'll be walking 'round here smelling shitty. 'Cause she can really smell like a li'l outhouse when she craps," she joked.

I changed her in no time and bounced her up and down on my lap. Sparkle came in the room wearing a hip hugging black mini dress that gripped her curvy frame and a pair of black six-inch platform wedges. She had her long bangs swept to the side, and hair pulled back and pinned to her head.

"You looking like a diva," I commented.

"So do you," she said back. "I see you're having fun with your niece's spoiled butt."

"She's a good baby."

Aunt Ruby chimed in, "Yeah, she is a real good baby. That's why I don't mind keeping her. I wouldn't fool with her if she was a big mouth holler box."

I stood and passed Layla to Auntie. I leaned over and gave her a kiss on her jaw. "I love you."

Sparkle walked over and kissed the baby on her forehead. "See you later, you li'l stinker," she kidded.

We walked out of the door, got in my car, and went on down the highway.

In an hour, we were parking in the parking lot of Silver Star hotel and Casino in Philadelphia,

Mississippi. In minutes, we were treading into the doorway on a Wednesday night. The inside of the place was loud with the sound of machines going off. The Casino housed at least 2,500 slot machines. A bunch of tables was set up with Craps, Blackjacks, Roulette, mini baccarat, and eight poker tables.

I pointed to the women's restroom. "Let's go in there real quick. I need to pee."

I led Sparkle into the room and took off to find an empty stall. I locked the door behind myself. I was using the bathroom when I heard someone throwing up vomit and choking on it. I got finished peeing, flushed the toilet, and pulled my dress down. I walked out and didn't see my sister anywhere in sight. I figured that she must've stepped back out until she came out of one of the stalls. I could tell she had been throwing up. As soon as she got up close to me I smelled vomit. "Heifer, are you pregnant?" I asked her.

"Yep." She ignored my mouth dropping down to my ankles and washed her hands and face off in the sink.

"By Ontavious?" I wanted to know.

"No, Sayveon," she mumbled.

"Lord have mercy," I said, shocked. "Well, damn. That means you can't drink tonight, but I'm gon' drink enough for both of us. I'm getting twisted." I looked at her facial expression. "You don't seem too happy about it."

"I'm not."

"Well, come on, and let's go to the bar for a li'l while. You can't drink, but I want to get buzzed. You can keep me company. If you start to feel sick again let me kno', and I'll take you home."

She dried her hands with a paper towel and used one of her hands to fan herself. "I'm starting to feel a li'l better."

I moved over to the bar area and the whole time I was wondering how Sparkle was going to deal with being pregnant by Sayveon when her heart was with Ontavious. She had gotten herself in a world of trouble this time.

About To Do The Unthinkable

Stephanie

There were about twenty men at the bar getting throwed and talking to each other. Most of them were watching the '52 inch flat screen TV on the wall that displayed a wrestling match. I had found me a company keeper and was drinking some Ciroc on ice. Sparkle sat watching the lightweight fight on the screen and ignoring the hell out of us both. She cupped her hand under her chin and asked the waiter if she could have a glass of soda. He immediately got her a drink and sat the glass in front of her.

"Thanks, sweetie," she told him. She sipped from the straw.

The dude beside me was an attractive chocolate like a brownie. He had the prettiest straight teeth and around 5'8 or 9. His deep baritone voice was so sexy.

"Have you hit the jackpot tonight?" I asked.

"I just hit it when you sat down beside me," he flirted.

"Aah. That's cute. You better not let your girlfriend here you say that," I hinted to see if he was rockin' it solo.

"I've been married for six years."

"I'm not really single, but I'm available tonight." I smiled.

Sparkle bumped my leg. "Damn. Y'all really are feeling each other, huh?"

I leaned over and mouthed, "He's cool people." She started back watching the huge tall baldhead white man on the TV wresting with another shorter guy who was white too with blue hair. The taller of the two tossed the shorter one all around the ring. I laughed hysterically at the match. Once the liquor hit my system, a lot of shit got funny. My newfound friend, Marcus, whispered in my ear. "I have a hotel here, and I would love for you and your sister to join me. Maybe we can have a trio." He chuckled behind his remark, but I knew he was serious as a heart attack.

He said earlier that he was a Criminal Defense Lawyer so I knew his money had to be long.

I nudged Sparkle. "This dude wants to have a threesome. He's gotta be drunk to ask me some shit like that," I murmured.

"Hell nah. I don't get down with that." She frowned and shook her head. "Nasty fucka."

I bumped her arm with my elbow. "Be quiet." She looked at me and quickly shook her head from side to side.

"I don't kno' what you plotting up, but ain't shit shakin' over here. You can kill yo' thoughts. Girl, you sick." She rolled her eyes and scooted over in her chair like I was infectious.

"Girl, yo' coochie prob'ly raggedy and all bent out of shape. I don't want you," I joked.

She waved me off. "Please. You must be thinking 'bout yo' own."

"Let's go to his room. He's full of that liquor and ready to trick off." I squirmed in the chair and pulled down my dress that was sliding up my thigh.

He wrapped his arm around my shoulder and moved my head to him. He whispered, "I'll give you five thousand dollars if you two will show me a good time."

Cha Ching! Hearing him say that had dollar signs in my head. Liquor gave me boldness and would gas me up to do shit that I normally wouldn't. I sure wasn't gonna lay down with him for free. He really wasn't my speed because there was nothing spectacular about him but his pockets. Besides, I could use the five stacks that he offered. I could hit the jackpot with him. It would be like stealing candy from a baby. I had to figure out a plan to get my bougie sister to come up there with me. Sparkle would be the only problem, but I had a game plan.

The Truth Comes Out

Sparkle

Things had really gotten stupid. I let Stephanie persuade me to go up to the man's room with her. I was only supposed to be the lookout person for her in case something unexpected went down. She was forever getting herself into some bullshit. Now, here she was dragging me into her craziness, and I kept my fingers crossed that this would all be over soon. I agreed that I would only watch out for her and stand by the door. If she screamed, or I heard anything foul going on, I was supposed to help her. Yeah, this was some off the wall ish that only Steph's pea-brain would conjure up. Little did she kno', but I was only agreeing to this because I needed a favor from her. I hadn't told her yet, but it was in the making.

I looked over at Marcus, and it was very noticeable that he was buzzing from the alcohol in his system. His speech was slightly slurred, and his eyes had turned red as a ruby. All three of us got off the elevator on the fourth floor and sauntered to his room. Stephanie reached in her purse, upped a pocketknife, and sneaked it to me when he wasn't paying attention. "If he acts a fool when we get up in here, slit his throat from ear to ear," she said.

"Hell nah. You keep it and cut him if he comes at you on some bullshit. I've already caught a case for slicing a broad up. I ain't trying to get in no more trouble," I let her know and gave it right back.

She stuck it in her bra. Marcus stuck the room key into room # 238, unlocked the door, and went on in. Me and Stephanie trailed behind him and I shut the door. I stood at the entrance and let Marcus and Stephanie go to the bedroom area. I heard her ask him for her money and seconds later I heard him count her out the exact amount he owed her. I had my back turned because I didn't want to see what they were about to do. I heard the television come on, and I was praying that the stupidity would be over as soon as possible. *Can't believe this heifer got me in here for this,* I thought to myself.

"Hey, how about you let your sister see me fingering you. That would really turn me on," I heard Marcus say.

"Nope, she's not down with that so come on and let's do what we came in here for," she said in a low tone. The next thing I heard were his pants being unzipped. Seconds had passed when I overheard the sound of sloppy wet noises from her giving him some head. It was sickening. The slurping noise of her sucking him and his moaning made me feel like I wanted to gag and puke all over the floor.

"What the hell you got goin' on?" Stephanie asked with a roar in her tone.

I tiptoed to the corner and peeped my head around the wall. I was making sure everything was gravy. The man had his hands over his penis area. She was struggling to force his hands loose from between his legs. She looked up and caught me staring.

"Girl, please, come help me pin his arms down," she begged.

I slowly went over because I wasn't sure what was going on, and I didn't want to get caught up in nothing stupid. My last altercation with that knife and the whole Nakia situation had me cautious. There were cameras at that hotel, and I didn't want to be charged with nothing else. I stood over him and asked her, "What are you doing to him?"

"Just trust me and do what I told you. He's hiding something."

I used my knee to hold his hand down so he couldn't move. I curved over to investigate the problem. "Well, I'll be damned." I gasped. The view was eye catching and almost knocked me off my feet.

It's All Come To The Light

Stephanie

I was stunned to see that Marcus was a hermorphidite. He had both a ding-a-ling and a coodie.

"Oh hell nawl. I'm 'bout to go," Sparkle blurted and headed for the door.

"No, Sparkle," I told her.

She twisted her body around suddenly. "What you 'bout to do?"

I placed my hand on my hip. "Get paid." I had one thing on my mind, and that was keeping the bread he'd given me. I figured it couldn't have been that bad. I had been on the mean streets for years when I was an addict. Therefore, nothing was too much for me to handle. My sister on the other hand, wasn't feeling it.

She stormed out of the door and said over her shoulder, "I'll be in the hallway."

"Let's get this over with so the both of us can walk away happy," I told him.

Marcus stood to his feet and pulled my dress over my head. He chuckled, a low, throaty sound that vibrated through my neck as he kissed the spot just under my ear. "I want you, and while I'd really like to take my time exploring this succulent body, that's going to have to wait for later." He loosened his grip and carefully placed my arms around his neck. He leaned in, his gaze so full of heated passion that I nearly melted at that moment. His lips touched mine and I couldn't stop the trembling that shimmered through my body. I hung on tightly as he nibbled at my mouth, barely registering his fingers at my waist. Then he slid his hand inside of my thongs, fingertips circled my sensitive bud as he pushed my underwear off my hips. He dipped one long finger into my wetness, then another, a moan flew from my mouth. This nigga was the shit!

I let my hands slide down his broad chest. My fingers rubbed his muscles and slowly fell down to his crotch. I massaged his length, nibbling along his neckline as I wrapped my hands around his dick. He was average, smooth, and oh so hard against my palm as I stroked him from base to tip. He groaned as he slid his fingers out and lifted me up. I wrapped my legs around his waist. He laid me on the bed and reached for his pants on the floor. Marcus pulled a condom from his wallet, took it out of the wrapper, rolled it up the head of his wood slowly, and climbed on top of me. Holding me tightly with one hand, he entered me in one long, smooth thrust.

I dropped my head back, my body thrummed with the intensity of unexpected emotion. I felt his lips on my breasts, moving up my collarbone and over my neck, and up to the tip of my chin. I raised my head slightly with my eyes closed and waited to feel his mouth against mine again.

"Open your eyes, Sweetheart," he voiced and I slowly did what he instructed. He pulsed inside of me. I met his gaze, shocked at the intensity staring back at me. "I love being inside of you."

"You got my pussy feeling so good," I whispered against his lips.

He rewarded me with a crushing kiss and began to move within me, spirals of pleasure rushed through my body. I closed my eyes once more, giving myself over completely to the feel of his lips moving down my neck, his body locked tightly to mine. I felt whole as if some part of me that had been missing was now restored. Moving with him, I matched the movements as I gave myself over to his passion.

The thrust came faster causing my body to become simultaneously tense and relaxed. The pressure was building like mad and a fuzzy warm tingle started in my toes. My breathing became heavy which was a sign that my orgasm was arriving and the best feeling in the world traveled from my kitty and landed all over him. He pumped a few more times before he uttered, "Oh, shit." He collapsed on top of me, hugged me against his chest, and kissed me on my neck. A tear fell down my cheek and I couldn't believe I was laying my ass up there crying. The shit felt so right that my eyes literally dripped water like a faucet.

"Are you okay," he wanted to know with a raised brow.

"I'm straight," I assured and used the back of my hand to wipe away the teardrops. "That was the best feeling I've ever had in my life. You made me cry like a baby." I let out a loud laugh, and he laughed along with me.

I gently stroked Marcus' waves in his hair a few times. He rolled off me and collapsed by my side. The minute his body hit the mattress, I heard a cracking noise.

"What the fuck?!" I yelled wondering what had just happened when we both landed on the floor after the bed broke. It scared me so bad that I almost pissed on myself.

"You good?" Marcus asked, lying beside me on the brown carpet. He stood and grabbed my hand to help lift me up and we got dressed quickly.

Once I was completely clothed, we exchanged numbers and embraced one another. I had just had a one-night stand, and I didn't feel guilty about it. I'd rather be paid to get laid rather than do it for free. The streets taught me that no matter what I did, I needed to make sure that I always looked out for me. I might've been a fool in the past, but I sure wouldn't keep being one forever.

Shit Getting Real

Sayveon

After my car was bombed, I tried to calm down and think. I scratched the back of my head while sitting out on the patio with Pops. I had asked myself over and over who would have done this shit. No names came to mind except dude who had shot Carmen and me, but that lame ass nigga wasn't gangsta enough to blow my car up. Whoever this was seemed to be on some Mafia business.

"Man, Pops, shit is gettin' crazy, and I'm gon' have to lay low until I find out what's goin' on," I told him.

He nodded and sat straight up in his chair. "Son, we will find out who's behind this and when we do, he'll pay with his life."

The doorbell rang breaking our conversation up. I stood and treaded to the front door. I looked out of a side window and saw two black male po-pos standing on the other side. "Shit," I whispered to myself. I hated law enforcement, and I sho' didn't feel like answering a hundred questions. My nose flared from aggravation, and I unlocked the door and cocked my head to the side like, *Nigga what?* About sixty people filled the streets gawking along with about five news reporters standing out there with their microphones in their hand. Flashing lights, blaring sirens, police, and fire fighters were everywhere in the street.

"We're looking for the person whose car this is," the taller of the popos stated and pointed over his shoulder.

"It's mine, why?" I asked. I looked around him and could see a female investigator taking pictures of the damage and the surrounding area. The taller one at the door had Officer T. Kennedy on his nametag. He jotted down everything that I had told him which wasn't much 'cause I didn't kno' nothing myself. Even if I had of known something, I wouldn't have told them. Didn't trust 'em and didn't like 'em.

"Mr. Travis, we're going to need as much detail as possible of when the car was damaged. Who do you think did it?"

"All I kno' is I heard a loud noise, came up to the door, and my shit was on fire."

He handed me a card. "This has your incident number on it. You should keep it and provide that to your insurance company. It's up to you whether or not you make a claim."

"Aight," I mumbled. They turned and walked away.

A young Caucasian reporter yelled, "Can you tell us why someone would set your car on fire?"

I shrugged and was about to close the door when she hollered out, "Sir, is there anything you would like to say?"

"Yeah." I nodded. She showed all of her pearly whites waiting for a response. "Fuck you! Nosey hoe!"

Her mouth slightly dropped and her face turned blush red. She dropped her small notepad on the ground, bent over to retrieve it, flicked her hair, and marched off. I slammed the door and stood there ear hustling.

"We're here at 312 Heritage Place where a car bomb exploded. Luckily, the blast injured no one. A man two blocks away says he heard the explosion from his house. Investigators found evidence that the bomb was detonatored with a cell phone. Federal Officers showed up at the scene after several residents called 911 and reported the incident. At this time, no arrest has been made. Regina Carl, Channel 11 News."

I moved away from the door and walked back where Pop was. I had some plotting to do, and I was about to set some shit off real soon.

On A Mission

Sayveon

I sauntered to the back where Pop was with a lot on my mental. I had to handle mine and handle it quickly.

"Pops, I'ma have to holla at you later. I need to make a run," I said standing in front of him.

He ran his hand in his pocket and upped his car keys. "Here, son, take my Beamer and bring it back whenever you get situated."

I accepted the key and turned to walk away. "Thanks. Good lookin' out."

He followed behind to the side door attached to the garage and closed it behind me. I stepped out into his three-car garage where he had three whips parked. His black '12 BMW was at the far left hand side. His '12 white Mercedes Benz E- Class and a new-modeled black Ford Expedition sat side by side. I hit the unlock button on the key chain for the Beamer and climbed behind the wheel. I had started the engine when I noticed that Pops had let the garage door up for me to exit. I reversed the car and backed out of the drive.

The media yelled out questions and mobbed the vehicle. All I could see were microphones pointing at the window and hear a bunch of questions being thrown at me. "Sir, can you tell us why someone would want to blow up your car?" a high-pitched feminine voice wanted to know.

"Can you tell me if you think someone has a hit on you or your family, Mister?" a deep voiced male reporter asked.

I geared the whip in drive, eased down on the accelerator, and drove down the street. I grabbed my cell out of the front of my jeans, scrolled down my contacts, and hit up my nigga, Rich.

"Sup, fam?" I greeted once he answered the phone.

"Chillin' at the crib 'bout to smoke on some Keisha. What you 'bout to get into?" He coughed a few times sounding like he was strangling. He was puffing on some good green.

"I'm 'bout to come through and holla at you on the business tip."

"I'm here."

"That's what's up. I'll holla at you in a few," I made known and pressed END and disconnected the call.

I turned the radio on to 99.7 and listened to the remix of The Game's tune blaring from the speakers 'Celebration' featuring Bone Thugs-N- Harmony. I bobbed my head to the beat while planning my next move. The music helped me think and the more I thought, the hotter I got. I had an issue wit' a nigga, and I finally got word of where he rested. I was mos' def' 'bout to bring some hell to heaven.

On my way to Rich's crib, I lowered the volume on the radio and hit my mom up on her house phone. She sweetly answered after the second ring. "Hello, my baby. How are you?" she greeted.

"I'm good. How you doing?"

"I'm alright. I'm sitting around here watching the world news. People are really doing a lot of killing now a day. Er' day somebody is being killed somewhere. You be careful because there are some fools out in this world," she warned me.

"I know. I watch my back; ain't got no worries." I switched subjects. "How Miss Sophia doing?"

"I talk to her every day, and she's turning seventy in a few more days. Her two daughters supposed to be throwing her a big birthday party. She's so excited about it, but she called me earlier complaining about her son Li'l Earl. You know his wife dropped him like a bad habit a few weeks ago. Sophia told me that the wife says he drinks all night and don't want to do nothing but run up behind a woman's skirt tail," she gossiped.

Hearing her give me a piece of the info I needed sounded good to my ears. I knew if anybody had the latest on what was going on in Crystal Springs, Mississippi, it was Mama. Miss Sophia was an elderly woman in the neighborhood and had been her best friend since I was a youngster. I suspected that her son had me set up at the club when I got caught slippin'. That's when they popped me and Carmen.

"Where he staying at now 'cause I saw him down here one night. It was a while back though."

"He's over there living with Sofia. He gets on my last nerve with that loud music that he plays. His car is an old box Chevy. I don't kno' what's the loudest his car or his radio. It sounds like it needs a muffler." She chuckled. "I know when he steps on his brakes too because they sound like a loud whistle when they screech. He's not working. He probably doesn't have the money to buy new brake pads. I don't blame his wife for putting his sorry ass out. Sofia said he's been over there sleeping all day. He was out all night and got pissy drunk," she chatted.

I was silent as I started to scheme. "Hello?" she said.

I came back to reality. "I'm here, Mama. I'm listening to you."

She yawned loudly. "I better get up and go on to choir practice before I get too sleepy to leave here." I heard her phone go out for a minute, which indicated that another call was tryna come through. "Hol' on for a minute."

She clicked over, and I hopped on Interstate 55. I mashed the gas and passed several cars trying to get to my destination quickly. Mama returned to my call.

"I'll talk to you later, baby. That was Sofia, and she ready for choir practice. I'm gon' pick her up and we goin' on. Call me again, and I love you."

"I love you, too."

I ended the call and tossed it over on the passenger's seat. Minutes later, I was rolling into Rich's driveway and spotted a familiar car. I murdered the engine and planted my Gucci sneakers on the ground. I heard talking coming from somewhere. I looked up and Nakia's sister, LaShune, was walking out of the door geared in a lil bitty white shirt, white and red coochie cutters, and a pair of white gym shoes.

She strolled down the pavement walking to her car while Rich stood in the door. She gave me a huge smile, puckered her mouth out, and kissed at me. Then she glided her tongue over her top lip. "What's up, Sayveon," she spoke before she turned to jump in her whip. Her pants were wedged in her ass crack and her cheeks hung out.

"What it do, Shawdy?" I knew ole' girl was a hoe only lookin' for a nigga to sponsor her. I knew for a fact that Rich wasn't the only dude she kicked it with, but that wasn't my place to say nothing. Plus, Rich was acting like she had him pussy whipped lately so I wasn't gonna rain on his parade.

Fam stood in the door watching her leave and grinning like he had a fly bitch, but really she was a thirsty trick.

"Come on in, homeboy," Rich said and went back inside his pad.

I stepped through the door and made my way into his den. He sat with a sack of loud in front of him and a cigarillo. He picked up the kush and started rolling.

"I came over here to tell you 'bout some shit," I told him sitting on the sofa. I leaned my head back and ran my hand down the side of my face. "Pops say that Jackie pregnant."

"Damn. Big Al still 'round here making babies. He the man, huh?" He smiled and split the 'rillo down the middle.

I leaned over and looked at him. "The baby ain't his. He says he had surgery to make him sterile. He wants us to hit Miami up and see what's goin' on wit' her. She's down there visiting her mama."

"Man, she way younger than he is. You kno' somebody gon' be puttin' some pipe to her. Then, they was living in two different states for the longest, but that's on him. If he want us to go, I'll go," he voiced and filled the 'rillo up. When he was done, he licked it to moisten it, grabbed a cigarette lighter off his end table, and dried the blunt before lighting it. He took a long puff off it and passed it to me.

I hit the blunt one good time and passed it back. This was exactly what I needed to ease my mind. "Gon' get right so we can ride out in a few. My car got bombed at Pops house, and I'm thinkin' dude who shot me may be after me. I may just be 'noid, but still I gotta murk him. Whether he behind the shit or not, I ain't gon' let him keep breathing. Somebody want me bruh, but I ain't had no beef wit' nobody," I said. I shook my head. "I don't kno' who behind this shit, but he gon' be body bagged when I catch him. I don't kno' if somebody larger than him ordered a hit on me or what the fuck goin' on."

"Yo' car got bombed?" He asked looking like he could hardly believe it. "Goddamn. I ain't never heard of no car bombings goin' on in The Sipp."

"Me either. I'm gon' stay low key til I find out what's goin' down. These mothafuckas done burned my house down, blew my car up, and there's no telling what's next. I'ma have to take whoever behind this out before they get me."

"You kno' where he be at?" Rich asked and grabbed the glock from the small table beside him and tucked it on his waistline. I could tell from the deadly look in his eyes that he was ready to ride out and spray dude.

"He just moved back wit' his mama, and that's my mama's neighbor. Let's roll 'cause his mama ain't home, and I don't want to hurt that old lady. I been knowing her all my life." I wasn't a killer til I was pushed to the limit, even then I promised myself that I would never kill a child or elderly person.

"Shid, granny can get it too." He smirked, but I ignored his comment and got up.

"Let's do this shit," Rich said sounding amped up. I asked him to get us both some gloves before we hit the highway. A mothafucka was 'bout to get his issue.

Once we made it to Crystal Springs and on the street where Mama lived, I slowed down. I wanted to scope the area out first before making any kind of move. The neighborhood was quiet. There were now only three houses on the street. The other two houses that were there when I grew up were now dilapidated. Mama had the best-looking house in that area. She and daddy had always taken pride in keeping their home up.

I pressed down on the brakes and looked at the house two times. "That's where he stay, right there." I pointed over to the spot. There was a driveway right beside the house. I remembered Ms. Sophia driving through there and parking her car in the back of the house when I was younger. I quickly snatched the car over, drove to the back of the house, and turned the headlights off. His white box Chevy was in the backyard so I knew he was inside. I sat in the darkness with the ignition on. I tol' Rich what to do and he got out of the car.

Rich pulled his gray hoodie over his head, put on his black gloves, and moved to the back door. He banged on it several times and couldn't get a response. I let the window down. "Go knock on the windows. That'll make him raise up." I exited the car too and waited on the side of the house while sliding my hands in the gloves. I could hear Rich knock on a few front windows, and then he knocked on the front door. I went over and ducked behind a big bush that was in the front yard.

"Who is it?" I heard his groggy voice holla out.

"Yo' mama tol' me to come get you," Rich lied. "Something happened at the church."

Li'l Earl came to the door and cracked it. "What's goin' on?"

Rich bomb rushed the dude and pointed his steel at his head. I jumped from 'round the bush and made my way inside after taking my iron off my waist. Li'l Earl was standing there looking like he'd just seen a ghost. "Why the fuck you have me set up?" I demanded.

He held his hands up like he was under arrest. "I ain't have nothin' to do wit' that, my nigga."

"Who had it set up then? You gon' tell me somethin'." I caught him off guard when my fist made contact with his stomach. His knees buckled from the force of the blow, and he doubled over. He went down to the floor and gasped for air. A yellow and brown substance erupted from his mouth along with some blood. He lay on his side like a helpless newborn. I raised my shoe and mercilessly stomped down on his face several times. He let out a loud groan.

"Shut the fuck up and stand," I ordered. He slowly stood holding his stomach. I looked over at Rich who still had his heater cocked on Li'l E. "Gon' put 'em to sleep." The minute the words came out I heard two rounds go off. I looked down and saw that he had two bullet holes, one in his jaw and another in his temple. Blood gushed from the wounds and leaked onto the floor. His eyes rolled far back into his head and a tear fell.

"Damn, I'm thirsty as hell," Rich said and went in another direction of the house.

"Where the fuck you goin', nigga," I snapped ready to bounce.

"My mouth is dry. I'm 'bout to see if they got a soda in the refrigerator real quick." I couldn't believe the nerve of this nigga. We had just blasted a dude, and he was worrying about finding something to drink.

Suddenly there were three knocks at the door. Me and Rich both froze in our tracks. After several minutes passed, the person knocked about five more times, hard.

I heard a chick holler, "Li'l E, open up this mothafuckin' door. Uh, huh, how you gon' tell me to come over while Ms. Sophia at choir rehearsal, and you up in here wit' some other hoe? Whose car is that parked behind the house?"

Rich upped his steel and crept into the hallway. I slowly stepped to the entrance and opened it. The female looked me up and down before asking, "Who the fuck are you, and where is E at?" She had a six-pack of beer in her hand and two big Wendy's bags. Ole' girl had to be at least three hundred pounds and favored the actor who played the role of 'Precious.'

"Who you?" I questioned her.

"His wife. Why you answering doors like you live here or..." I grabbed her around her shoulders. I snatched her inside before she could speak another word, but she was overpowering me. She tossed her arms in the air and the two bags tumbled to the steps spilling fries and hamburgers. She used all of her weight and pinned me against the wall.

"You asshole. Don't you be puttin' yo' goddamn hands on me. What the hell you trying to do? You ain't gon' rape me," she said, but I didn't want no parts of her meaty pussy.

She turned toward me and connected her knuckles to my jaw. Her balled fist came towards me the second time, but I blocked the blow with my arm. She scratched and kicked me in the knee, and I almost hit the hardwood floor. She drew blood from my arm with her sharp fingernails. I knew I had to bring the noise with this big Sumo wrestler. The chick was going ape. I punched her one good time in the face, and she fell backwards.

Her attention fell on Li'l E for the first time and her bottom lip trembled. "You killed my husband!" she screamed to the top of her voice.

Rich aimed his burner at her and was laughing at the same time. "She almost beat you like you had stolen something. Damn, bruh, you had to bring the heat for this big mothafucka."

She raised up one hand. "Stop, please don't do this. I'll give y'all whatever you want. Just don't kill me. I got two kids at home that I'm not ready to leave behind," she pleaded, but Rich stood over her and fired two shots into her dome. I watched her body shake uncontrollably before stopping. Blood oozed from her mouth and toppled to the wood floor. We dipped, leaving no witnesses.

Dealing With Reality

Sparkle

On the way home, I couldn't get the thought of being pregnant off my mind. I was stressed to the max thinking about the whole situation. My mind traveled to Sayveon wondering what his good for nothing ass was up to. I shook my head thinking that he was probably poking some new bitch with his cheating, lying self. I once believed that over the years he would mature and be ready to settle down without all of the immature nonsense. Boy, I was wrong and foolish. I guess when I was younger I had dreamed of a life much different from what I had settled for. By my mother and father being married for over thirty years, I wanted to follow their footsteps. Hmph, I had the right plan, but the wrong man.

I snapped out of my thoughts when I heard Stephanie say, "Girl, what you over there thinking about?"

"Nothing really."

"Stop lying. Your mind is somewhere because you haven't said a word since we've been in the car," she replied and looked over at me for a split second.

"I'm just upset about being pregnant," I revealed and let out a long sigh. "I went over to his crib today, and the white girl was over there talking shit and acting like she's his wifey."

"You don't need to go back over there. Leave that no good nigga alone and move on with your life. You have a new man, and you need to be more concerned about how you're going to tell him that you're having another man's baby. Ooh, I feel sorry for you because you are in some real talk show drama." She laughed before continuing. "Have you decided when you're going to tell him?"

I stared out of the window into the darkness. "Nope."

My cell phone started vibrating. I grabbed it from inside my purse and saw that it was Aunt Ruby's number flashing across the screen. Before I could say "hello," her mouth was going a hundred miles per hour. "Chile, is yo' baby's daddy named Seattle, Savior, or something like that? I can't ever pronounce his name good," she mumbled.

I giggled a bit. "His name is Sayveon," I slowly and clearly said into the receiver.

"Well, that's the name. Girl, I was sitting up here watching the nine o'clock news on Channel 40, and he was on there. Somebody blew his car up earlier today, and he almost ran over a few of the camera people backing up out of the yard. Now, he's a fool, and I'm glad you got out from down there with him. Somebody must be after him," she speculated. "The news woman said his name was Sayveon Travis. And that someone tipped them off saying that it was his car that was set on fire and the right sources confirmed it."

"Was he a dark chocolate color with dreadlocks in his hair?" I asked, thinking that she must have had the wrong person."

"He had something that looks like braided long snakes in his hair. Yeah, that's what y'all young folks call dreadlocks."

My heart almost stopped pumping. I kept thinking of how the house was put on fire before I left him. I was glad that I had removed myself from his crib and moved on because he was living a dangerous life that I didn't want to be a part of. I wanted more for me and my daughter. I had dreams for her one day being a productive young woman. In addition, Sayveon's lifestyle wasn't what I wanted her to be around, and I surely didn't want her to follow in his footsteps. The sound of Auntie's loud voice knocked me out of my daze.

"Are you on the phone? Hello?" she said.

"I am still here. I'm shocked that all of this has happened."

"Well, it will come back on the ten o'clock news; you better come on if you don't want to miss it."

"I'm on my way now. I'll see you in a little bit."

"Y'all be careful on that highway. The deer are out and almost taking over at night."

"Okay, bye."

I disconnected the call with the press of a button and rested my head back on the seat.

"What was all of that about?" Stephanie wanted to know.

"Sayveon. Auntie says that he was on the TV. Somebody bombed his car. I want to see it. It's coming on again on the ten o'clock news."

"Damn, he's getting all of his dirt back and he's getting it back quick," she added.

I nodded. "I was going through his phone earlier and saw where he has gotten Pops daughter, Carmen, pregnant. She's his sister."

"What kind of crazy shit is that? And, what you mean that Pops' daughter is his sister?" she inquired holding her right hand over her chest as if she was about to have a heart attack.

"Pops is Sayveon's daddy. I haven't been around you to give you the whole scoop on that stupid family."

"That's a shame before God," she let out shaking her head.

Switching the topic I asked, "I need you to go to the doctor with me in the morning. I'm going to need all of the support I can get."

We chatted back and forth until we got to Auntie's house. Stephanie promised to pick me up and take me to my appointment. I was glad that she had turned her life around and gotten off drugs. She was now acting like the big sister that I wanted and needed her to be. It was comforting to know that I had someone on my side that cared about my well-being.

Me and my sister both got out of her ride and strutted inside of Aunt Ruby's place five minutes before ten o'clock. Layla was asleep on her lap so I picked her up and laid her down in my bed and walked back into the living room where the two of them were seated. The news soon came on, and I was anxious to hear about Sayveon and the ordeal that went down earlier. After it went off, I sat there stiff as a board wondering who he had made mad this time. I said a silent prayer for him, but he was only getting back everything that he had issued over the years. Payback is a bitch, and someone must be feeling some sweet revenge right now.

Some People Can't Be Changed

Stephanie

As I drove down the highway headed home, I kept thinking about my past. I had come so far and was actually proud of myself. Two years ago, I would have never dreamed that I would be drug free and doing well. It was my intention to never touch any more heroin. I was clean, and I planned to stay that way. As long as I kept the right people around me who had a positive impact in my life, I'd be fine.

I pulled into the apartment building's parking lot and parked next to James' truck. I hopped out and pressed the car alarm on my key chain. When I got to the door, I put my key in the lock and unlocked it. I made my way inside and noticed that James was in the living room with the television on. He jumped when he saw me. When I saw what he was doing, I was beyond disappointed. He held an insulin syringe in his hand and a belt was tied around his arm. He was about to shoot up.

"I thought you said you were done with that shit?" I asked him and closed the door behind me. I stepped over to the sofa staring at him.

He dropped his head. "Baby, I'm sorry. I'm stressed out. I got laid off from my job today."

"So, that has led you to start back doing drugs?" I asked in a motherly manner.

"This is the only way that I can forget about my problems. Don't come in here trying to lecture me on what I'm 'bout to do. Go on to the bedroom and go to sleep," he ordered.

"I really wish you would think about what you're about to do and change your mind," I tried to persuade.

Ignoring me, he injected the needle into his vein as I stood and watched. The temptation was hard, but I shook it off and proceeded into the bedroom, showered, and went back to check on James. He sat there fidgeting and scratching his body. I turned and walked away feeling like the world was on my shoulders. I tossed and turnedthat night from what I had seen James doing earlier. The only thing I could do now was pray for the strength to remain strong and not start back doing the drug myself.

The Next Morning

Sayveon

I woke up to the bright Mississippi sun streaming through the window. I rolled over and let out a loud yawn. I dreaded getting out of my bed so early to take Carmen to the abortion clinic, but I knew it was something that I couldn't back out of doing. I checked my cell phone that was lying beside me. I had five missed calls from Carmen, a text message, and two missed calls from my mother. I read Carmen's text that said, "I'll be ready when you get here and let me know when you're on your way." I planned to call my mom later on in the day. I tossed the covers aside and sat up rubbing my heavy eyelids. I stood to my feet and went into the bathroom to take a shower before getting dressed.

I tossed my boxers and t-shirt into the dirty clothes hamper, turned on the showerhead, and jumped in. After handling my hygiene, I put on a pair of dark indigo Kenneth Cole jeans, a white Polo, a fresh pair of all white low-top Jordan's, and let my dreads fall down my back. I stepped over to the dresser and sprayed the cologne, Reaction by Kenneth Cole, on my neck. I grabbed the car keys and was about to dip when I heard the doorbell ringing. I moved to the door and asked, "Who is it?" Nobody responded. I opened the door and looked down. My eyes spotted a brown box. I leaned over, picked it up, and came back inside.

I ripped the tape from the box and opened it. A skull that favored a dog's was inside. The long and sharp teeth verified that it was a dead dog's head. I dropped the box. The head fell out and rolled across the floor before stopping. I noticed a dog collar was around its neck with words on the tag. I walked up closer, bent over, and read what was on it. It had my name and address on it. I peeped over in the box and noticed that a note was inside too. I reached inside and read the paper that said, "You're a dog, and you deserve to die."

I kicked the head back into the box with no return address and left it outside in my backyard. That was some ill shit. Somebody was a sick mothafucka to send that to my door. Don't get me wrong, I was a street nigga, but that right there had me a li'l shook. I was dealing with somebody that had a mind issue and was after me fa real. I soon got myself back together, turned on the home security system, and bounced. I rarely ever used the alarm, but now I was glad that I had it installed. I knew that I had an enemy somewhere but still didn't know the culprit. I had already murked dude that set me up at the club. I couldn't think of nobody else I had issues with.

The drive to Carmen's apartment was long and full of anxiety and anger. I was gonna find out who was behind that threat even if I had to die trying.

I was maybe ten minutes from Carmen's apartment when my cell went off. I wasn't in the mood to talk to anybody at that point because any and everybody was suspect in my eyes. I pulled the phone from my pocket and saw that it was my mom hitting me up.

I answered, "Hello."

She started. "Boy, it's some foolishness going on around here! Somebody went over to Sophia's last night and killed her boy and his wife is in critical condition. The doctor's aren't sure she'll pull through but they are trying to do all that they can to help her." She sounded afraid and I could hear her sniffling.

"They don't kno' who did it?" I questioned like I was really interested. I was spooked because if she made it she could give a description of how me and Rich looked.

"No, they are still investigating. I'm half scared to stay in here by myself at night now. Sophia spent the night over here last night because she didn't want to be over there. That was her only son. She's going through hell right now. She cried all night long. And another thing, why were you on TV last night? All of my gossiping ass church members were looking upside my head and whispering to each other. The choir director is the one who told me that somebody blew your car up," she spoke with a concerned tone mixed with fear.

"Mama, I don't know who did it but I'ma be okay. I don't need you worrying over me."

"You're my child so of course I'm going to be worried to death over you."

"It's all good on my end."

"All good? Shit, it sounds like it's all bad if somebody blew your car up," she said disagreeing with my comment.

"I'll be alright. You just keep those doors locked over there where you are, and I'll come by to check on you soon. If you hear a new report on dude's wife, call me and let me kno'. I sho' hope she pulls through," I lied.

"I will call you if anything changes about her condition and I will talk to you later son. I love you."

"Love you too, Mama."

I ended the conversation and tossed my cell on the passenger seat. I was gon' have hell on my hands if ole' girl lived. I couldn't understand how she could have been still breathing after the bullet that Rich put up in her. Now I had some new shit to stress over added to what I already had going on with Carmen and the dog's head that arrived at my doorstep. It seemed like I couldn't catch a break to save my life.

I wheeled into The Briars Apartments in North Jackson off I-55 and pulled right up to Carmen's apartment door. She bounced outside wearing a black Maxi dress and a pair of black bob shoes. She plopped down on the seat. "You were supposed to text me when you were on the way," she said. I didn't respond because I had too much other shit goin' on. "Are you okay?" she asked out of concern.

"I'm straight."

She switched subjects, "I forgot you were driving my dad's car. He told me what happened at his house the other day with your vehicle. Speaking of vehicles, how do you like mine?" She pointed to a fresh vanilla- white drop-top Mercedes Benz SL-Class. She smiled. "You like it?"

I nodded. "That's real fly right there." I flipped the conversation. "Why you got an apartment if you going to school in January?"

"I just didn't want to live with my mom and dad until then. I'm sure Rich wants his own privacy too, so I moved in over here. Plus, I will still come back here on weekends and breaks."

I left that subject alone because Pops had enough bread to buy up the whole complex if he wanted to. I was sure that the money he was spending once a month on her place wasn't putting a dent in his pockets. I mashed down on the accelerator and drove off. The ride was a quiet one and the only sound was the radio playing on 99 Jams. My cell started to ring, so I reached over by Carmen's leg and retrieved it. My mom's number popped up on the screen. I answered, "What's goin' on, Mama?"

"I got some bad news. Li'l E's wife passed away a few minutes ago. The doctors couldn't save her. I feel so sorry for Sophia and for her kids," she sympathetically told me.

"She's in a better place," I let out. Deep down inside, I was glad she didn't make it through cause she would have snitched us out and had the po pos all over us.

"Yes, they both are. I hope they had their ducks in a row and can live in glory forever. If they hadn't accepted Jesus as their personal Lord and Savior then they are up shit creek without a paddle," she explained.

I wasn't into the whole religious thing so I rushed her off the phone. "I'll hit you back later and be easy."

"Okay, bye and remember to be safe."

"I will." I hung up.

A few minutes later, I exited off on the Woodrow Wilson exit before turning on North State Street. Once I made a right on Fondren, I spotted the pink stucco building with the pink roof. The street was packed with protesters holding signs and screaming at the young women entering the clinic.

A security guard directed me to park in the back of the building.

"You're all just killers, and you're going to rot in hell," one protester yelled out to a young white girl who went inside the clinic.

A group of black chicks walked by one of the female protesters who was yelling and screaming insults. One of the girls hollered back, "Go to hell. You ain't in my shoes, and you ain't gon' be the one up rocking and singing lullabies every night, so shut the hell up, hoe!"

"You are a murderer and there is a special place in hell for you," the protester struck back.

"Well, I will see you there, mothafucka!"

The protester rolled her eyes, stepped away, and sat back down in the lawn chair she brought with her. I hopped out and headed toward the door with Carmen who seemed to be uncomfortable with the talk that was coming at her.

"Ma'am, are you sure you want to kill your baby?" someone asked her.

I looked over at the older Caucasian woman. "Man, back the fuck up and get out of her business," I said to her. After that, she was quiet and only shook her head.

I opened the door for Carmen and didn't make eye contact with anyone. I had to sign my name on a piece of paper stating that she had someone to drive her home. After showing my license, I whispered in her ear, "I'm 'bout to go. You can call me when you're ready."

She said lowly, "I think I'm going to get the abortion pill, so I won't have to go through the surgical procedure."

"That's on you." I reached in my pocket, gave her five one hundred dollar bills, and turned to leave out the door when I spotted two familiar faces. Sparkle and her sister were sitting there in the cut looking right upside my head. Sparkle's nose flared, and her sister's eyes ran up and down my physique. If looks could kill, I would have been in the morgue with a tag on my toe. I pushed the door and was off to my car.

When I opened my car door, I heard a voice calling me. "Sayveon, you ain't shit, and I know damn well you didn't get your own fucking sister pregnant did you?" I turned around and there Sparkle was all in my personal space. Everybody in the parking lot that was going in the building turned around staring at me. Man, she had embarrassed the hell out of me and put my business all in the streets.

"Sparkle, now ain't the time or the place, and I ain't doing this with you today," I grumbled and sat down inside the ride and was about to close the door. Well, that was until she snatched the door and started with the bullshit.

"I'm not done talking to you. You should be ashamed of yo' self. Pops just don't know how grimey you are, and if I was as dirty to you as you have been to me, I'd tell it," she threatened.

"And if you do, you better leave the state cause I'll dig my foot all up in yo' ass," I firmly spoke.

"Boy, hush. You disgust me, and you gon' get yours sooner than you think. Cause you can't do wrong and think you gon' get away with it."

"I think you should have discussed yo' situation with me before you came up here. If that's my baby, I don't want you here. It must be the other nigga's," I said, trying to get the spotlight off me and the fucked up shit I had done with Carmen.

"Please. This is my body, and I'm no longer yo' woman, so I can do whatever I damn well please." She slammed the car door and walked away.

Now I had to worry about her running her mouth, and this getting back to Pops. Nevertheless, I trusted Sparkle. She had never betrayed me in the past, so I let it go and crept off. A skinny male protester held up a picture of a small fetus and stood in front of my ride, and I couldn't move. "Don't let your girlfriend do it," he yelled out.

"Get the fuck out my way," I shouted out of my window. Ignoring my command, he still stood there with his sign and wouldn't move. Then, some big ass oranges were being thrown and hit every car that pulled out from the clinic's parking spaces. What the fuck?!!

I looked upward to where they were coming from and heard a voice scream, "Repent, bastard." A young white dude in his mid twenties was in the huge magnolia tree talking shit.

I jumped out of the ride. "Mothafucka, climb down out of that tree, so I can beat yo' ass. Evidently, you don't know who I am, but you 'bout to find out."

Dude licked his tongue out at me and was making silly faces. He tossed another flying fruit my way, and it hit me on top of the head. This time it was a biggo grapefruit. "Goddamn," I hollered and rubbed the top of my head with the palm of my hand. I grabbed the grapefruit from the ground and threw it back at him. It socked him dead in the eye. I reached for the orange and popped him again. Yeah, I played baseball when I was younger and had a mean arm on me. The youngster lost his balance, and his feet dangled from the tree. I walked over to him, jumped, and reached for his leg and snatched him down. When he crashed to the ground, I gave him a right blow to the cheek. Several of the protesters yelled for me to leave him alone.

A fly, honey colored chick that was behind the car I was driving got out of her whip and came toward me. "He threw a grapefruit at my damn car too, and he better be glad it didn't put a dent in my hood," she said. She walked up on him and kicked him in the side. "Yo' mammy should have taught you some manners."

She marched back to her ride. I got in the car, and we both took off. I needed to fire up some loud after dealing with all of that. Really, I was disappointed in Sparkle for wanting to kill my seed. In the end, I knew she'd eventually get tired of my doggish ways and lose feelings for me. However, I still believed that one day we would find our way back to one another.

Bringing Out The Beast

Sayveon

Since the burning of Nakia's daycare, she was at home every day until she was able to find a new spot for her business. I hadn't heard from her in a good minute, so I decided to fall through and see what she had going on. When I made it in front of her crib, I found a black Dodge Charger sitting in the driveway. I assumed it was one of her sister, LaShune's, ducks that tricked off on her. I pulled in behind the whip, hopped out, and made my way up to the front entrance. After two knocks, Nakia popped up at the door and cracked it.

"What's up, Sayveon?" she asked with an attitude wearing a pink robe. She eye searched me from head to toe and looked nervous.

"Open the goddamn door. Whatchu got a nigga in there or something? What's the deal?" I wanted to know. I pushed the door all the way open and forced my way in. I looked over by the den and noticed that the television was on and a dude was sitting down on the couch. I walked in that direction. Dude looked up, saw me coming, and quickly stood to his feet. He was lean and stood about 6'1. I could tell from his clothes and the way he carried himself that he was a lame and wasn't from the streets.

He spoke. "What's up?"

"Who you?" I asked.

"I'm her husband," he made known and quickly glanced over at Nakia who stood in the doorway leaned against the wall with her arms folded.

Nakia cut in, "We were only in here talking. Ain't nothing going on."

With a look of confusion, the husband blurted, "What do you mean there is nothing going on? You told me you weren't dating anyone, so why are you explaining this to him. You just sat here and told me that the two of you were done." He pointed his finger at her. "You're going to explain what's going on here with you two, and you're going to explain it now."

She waved him off. "Be quiet and sit down. I've already told you about Sayveon, so stop being dramatic."

He stepped in her face. "You told me that you were no longer seeing him. Is this why we can't get back together? Is he the reason that you are determined to stay single? He's why you want a divorce, huh?" He grabbed her by the arms and shook her.

She pushed him off her. "Get away from me!" she screamed.

"Why have you been lying, Nakia?" he grilled.

"I haven't lied to you about anything. He hasn't really been coming around like that, but you know that I have told you about him." She turned away from him and moved over by the television.

"I'm gone. I ain't got time for this bullshit," I grumbled and was about to turn and bounce.

"No, you don't have to go anywhere. I will go, but I'm not done with you," he said, threatening Nakia who looked away from him and stared out of the window that she faced. He stared at me and said, "You have destroyed our family. You've stolen my wife and she's pregnant with our child."

My lip went upward and a frown popped up on my face. What the fuck?!! "Whatchu mean your child?" I questioned him and cocked my head to the side waiting for his response.

"She's pregnant with my baby," he told me with a raised brow.

"Damn, hoe! Whose baby you having?" I had to know.

Nakia smacked her lip and said, "Sayveon, you know this is your baby. Don't believe anything that this fool says. He's obsessed with me. Don't pay him any attention."

"I'll see you again," dude told her and marched out of the door and got ghost.

"Listen, if you knew you still wanted to see dude all you had to do was tell me. You got me coming over here for this bullshit and got dude saying that's his baby you 'bout to have." My hands went into the air, and I regretted coming over to see her. "You can go ahead and have whoever baby you pregnant wit', but I don't think that its mine."

She jumped in my face. "Now, don't you start. You know this is your baby. Don't even try it."

Tired of the lies and drama, I decided to go. I walked to the door, and Nakia came and blocked the entrance. "You're not going anywhere until we have a long talk. My husband has a serious mind problem. Don't believe anything that he says," she tried explaining, but I grabbed her arm and tossed her from in front of the entrance. She bounced right back where she stood before blocking me from leaving. "I'm telling you that he's a nutcase. I left him because we were two different people, and I felt so unhappy being with him. He's a nice man, but he's not the man for me."

My eyes went toward the ceiling and landed back on her, uninterested in her explanation. "Tell this shit to somebody else 'cause I ain't tryna hear it."

She placed her hand on my shoulder. "I think you should be more understanding. Don't forget how Sparkle stepped onto my property and showed out. I was left bleeding and sent away with the paramedics. Do you ever stop to think how that made me feel?"

"Don't try to game me. Move out the way so I can go."

She gazed into my eyes like she hadn't heard a word that I had said. My temper was rising, and I had to show her that I wasn't the one to be played wit'. She musta thought I was as weak as the dude she married. I wrapped my hand around her neck and pushed her into a wall, opened the door and got ghost. With all of that behind me, I was determined not to get caught up with no mo' bitches and all the extra shit. I was starting to see that nobody could be trusted, no niggas and no bitches.

The Day Of Counseling

Sparkle

I went back into the clinic and flopped down in the chair next to my sister. I snatched the papers that she was holding and finished filling out my paperwork.

Stephanie leaned over and whispered, "Girl, that boy ain't shit, and I'm glad you left him alone. Now I see why you wanted me to come here with you. You're making the right choice. Ask God to forgive you and keep it moving."

My emotions made water develope in my eyes. I was feeling bad about my decision, but I knew it was for the best. I began reading the questions and writing in my contact information, medical history, and other important information. After I was done, I turned the information in to the receptionist. I sat back down and started to look around at the other faces. There were about thirty of us mostly black and maybe six white females. The ages ranged, and we all had the same look, of embarrassment and sadness.

The television mounted on the wall was on the movie channel, Lifetime. Tears were falling down a young brown skinned girl's cheek as she sat holding her head down. She looked to be about fourteen or fifteen. An older woman, who I guessed was the mother, wrapped her arms around the girl's shoulder. My heart went out to the young female, and I was happy that I had Layla at a more mature age and didn't have to endure making the decision that she had made.

Carmen was seated to my right holding her head down. I assumed that she was trying her best not to make eye contact with me. Li'l hot pissy ass was preggos by Sayveon. It was ridiculous.

Stephanie elbowed me after I had looked off. When I glimpsed over at her, she nodded toward Carmen who held her head up. "She needs her ass whooped, and Sayveon does too," Stephanie said to me. She looked at her. "Baby, you're at the right place. Really, you should have been the first name on the list because being knocked up by yo' brother ain't cute."

Several of the women looked at Carmen.

Carmen rolled her eyes, shook her head, and blurted, "Fuck you, bitch. You don't know who my baby is by."

Stephanie crossed her leg. "Girl, please. Everybody knows that you were giving yo' goodies up to Sayveon. Pops thinks you're an angel, but you're just an undercover hoe."

Carmen popped her lips, looked away, and didn't utter another word.

I heard my name being called and quickly jumped to my feet and strutted behind the nurse. She took me into a room to do my blood work before I was directed to undress in another room, and I did a pelvic exam and ultrasound. One mind told me to keep my baby, but my other mind told me that I was making the best decision for myself. I laid on that table feeling like I was committing one hundred sins at the same time. I relaxed and kept telling myself that Sayveon wasn't ever going to change and I'd be a fool to bust my legs open to give birth to another child by him. I closed my eyes and kept thinking that I would be glad when all of this was over.

"Okay, you can get dressed and go in the first room to your left where you should see other young ladies. Someone will come in shortly and have a counseling session with you. You will be able to ask any questions or tell them of any concerns that you may have."

"Thank you."

I had gotten dressed and found my way to the counseling room where other females were. As soon as my bottom touched the seat, I found myself thinking that the universe intended for me to see Sayveon and Carmen at the clinic. The odds were zero to none that I would be there the same exact day that they were. It was a big coincidence. To me, it was a sign from a higher being, and I was paying close attention. Boy, was I a happy soul that I hadn't gone back to that devil.

My New Friend

Stephanie

My cell phone vibrated on my leg as I waited up front. An unknown number showed up on my screen. I answered on the first ring in my sexy voice.

"Hello."

"Yes, is this Stephanie speaking?" the male voice questioned.

"Yes it is, and who is this?" I took a deep breath, wondering who was on the other end.

"This is Marcus, baby. How have you been?"

I smiled and let out a girlish giggle. "I have been doing good. What's up with you?"

"I'm calling you from my work phone. I was sitting here thinking about you. I wanted to know what you have planned for tonight."

I licked my top lip and became silent for a minute. I had to think of a lie to tell James, but that wouldn't have been a hard task. "I'm sure I can. What time are you talking about?"

"I'd like to see you around eight o' clock. Let's meet at Olive Garden off of 55. Is that fine with you?"

"Okay, I'll see you then, Marcus."

"Alright, baby girl. I'll be in a cranberry-red Benz."

"Gotcha. Bye, Sweetie," I said before hanging up. I was more than happy that he had called. I planned to enjoy the night. I needed to get out of the house, and I had some deep decisions that I had to make later on. I did not intend to go back to drugs, but I knew if I continued to be around James, I'd be tempted to go back to my old lifestyle. I wanted to win and winning meant that I wouldn't be fucked up again with heroin.

I held my head back, and the old life that I once lived came flashing back through my head. I remembered how I slept with several men in order to get drug money.

My family was my everything, but I hadn't been a good mother and I was finally starting to be able to have a relationship with my boys. Trying to find my way back into their life was rough, but I felt blessed that things had gotten better. Their father had made extreme progress too, but now I had started to see that we would soon need to go our separate ways. If he didn't change for the better, I had every intention on walking away.

Facing My Worst Fear

Sparkle

Dang, I was happy to be finished with the counseling session, and I finally walked out and into the front where my sister was. I cracked a smile.

"Let's go," I told her on my way out of the door.

I racked my brain wondering where the hell Carmen went because she never came into the counseling room. Then I guessed that she had to have requested the abortion pill that would be the only reason that she wouldn't have been in the same room with me. When I was having my lab work done, I overheard the nurse direct a girl who was getting the pill to go to a small room in the opposite direction from the one where I was seated. That was just like Sayveon. He probably persuaded her to take the pill so he could hurry up and get rid of their little problem. He was most likely grinning in Pops face like he hadn't done a thing in the world. Little did Pops know, he had boned his daughter. What a shame.

I stepped out into the slightly cool fall weather and placed my Gucci shades over my eyes. I proceeded to the car with Stephanie beside me.

"Girl, I saw Sayveon come back to get his li'l tramp from here," Stephanie informed.

"I'm not surprised by shit that he does," I grumbled.

"You're nothing but sluts and you're going to rot in hell," the crazed white guy yelled from a tree. I heard some talking behind me and glanced over my shoulder. The group of young women who were in counseling too was walking behind me. The guy dug into the green bag he had. "Hey, whore. You're the devil," he said before lobbing a grapefruit at Stephanie's head.

"Aah, shit," she yelped out in pain. She rubbed her forehead with the palm of her hand.

It amused the protester so much that his loud laugh echoed through the air. Well, that was until he spotted the blue lights come to the scene. Two black officers pulled over and got out of the car. "Sir, you need to come out of the tree right now," one of the police ordered him.

The fruit thrower gradually came down from the tree and was arrested. The officer placed him in the back of the patrol car.

The other officers ruled, "I'm going to need you all to grab your belongings and move out of the street. You're causing a disturbance, and you all need to move away from this location." The protesters packed their belongings, gathered up all the signs, and did as the officer said.

I rubbed Stephanie's shoulder. When I saw one of the police approaching us I whispered, "Do you want to press charges against him for hitting you?"

She shook her head a little. "Nope, I'm gonna be okay. You kno' I don't do cops."

I led her to the car. "Do you want me to drive?"

"I'm alright. I can make it."

She used the remote on the keychain to unlock her doors, and I jumped in, ready to go. I was worn out from everything that had gone on that morning. Seeing Sayveon with Carmen had me exhausted, sickened, and heated all at the same time. And the fact that an dumb ass had hit my sister hadn't made the morning any better. I hoped that things wouldn't continue to spiral out of control because I didn't know how much more I could take.

"My head is killing me," Stephanie complained, rubbing the spot on her head.

"I'm sorry. I didn't know that fool would be stupid and hit you with a damn grapefruit." I glanced over at her and could see where the knot was rising. It looked similar to a milk dud. "Girl, that's not looking so hot right now," I said and pointed at the swelling.

"I know. I had a date tonight. I will call and cancel it. This is so fucked up." She slowed down for a red light and quickly glimpsed at the mirror. "Awl, goddamn. This looks too bad." She let out a long sigh and pouted.

"It's really not that bad. You should just wear a bang and go on. And, who in the world are you going on a date with James?" I presumed.

"Hell no. I'm going with Marcus. He's the dude from the casino." She smiled before releasing a chuckle.

"Oh goodness." I frowned and turned my head. "So, you're about to start dating him or her or whatever it is?"

"Don't start, and he is a man. He can't help it if he was born with both," she defended Marcus.

"Do what you do, but what about James? You are wrong because that man has changed his life and turned things around for both of y'all. You're living in a nice place in Ridgeland, and he's working and going to school. You should really be ashamed of yourself," I scolded. I looked at her like she was a few clowns short of a circus, meaning dumb as hell.

The traffic light suddenly turned green. She eased down on the accelerator and refocused her attention to the street. She blew out a lot of air and I could tell from her gesture that I struck a nerve. "Please, don't start with that bullshit about how James has changed because I don't want to hear it."

"What's yo' problem?" I looked upside her head because her attitude was funky.

"I wasn't gonna say nothing, but I caught him getting high last night when I came home. He's been laid off, and he said he was doing it because he was stressed out," she was able to say before she choked on her words. A tear dropped from her eyes. She used the back of her hand to wipe the water away. She continued, "I don't want to go back to that life. I don't even want that shit around me. I'm trying to be strong, but how can I when he's doing the very thing that I'm afraid of?"

I rubbed up and down her back to comfort her. "You're going to be alright. Do you think you need to move out?"

"I don't know, but I do know that I can't stay there with that or I'll end up going back." Her hand trembled on the steering wheel. "It was so hard for me not to run that needle in my arm."

"Pull over," I quickly demanded. She whipped into the parking lot of The University Hospital. I opened the door and leaned my head down toward the gray concrete pavement. Vomit exploded from my throat, and all of my sausage and biscuit from that morning escaped from my mouth. I coughed and choked on my breakfast. After a few minutes, my stomach was empty. My breathing grew heavier.

Stephanie handed me some napkins from the console. I wiped my mouth and leaned my head backwards on the seat. I was sicker with this baby than I had been with Layla. I was so sick I could barely think straight. I could hardly wait for my appointment the following morning. I rested my eyes and soon drifted off. I wished that I could sleep away all of my problems, but I knew that was impossible.

Skeleton's Out Of The Closet

Sparkle

My mind was fuzzy, and the last thing I remembered was the scary dream I had. It was something about someone shooting Sayveon in the head, but the details quickly faded when I tried to recall them. Ugh, I couldn't even keep that mothafucka out of my dreams, and he quickly turned 'em into nightmares. I couldn't stand his ass. With a mental sigh, I allowed my brain to focus and opened my eyes. We had made it to Aunt Ruby's place, and my sister killed the engine.

"You need me to help you get out?" she asked with concern.

"I think I'll be okay." I got out, stood, and heard my cell alerting me that a text had come through. I rambled in my purse and pulled it out. I had a text from Ontavious that said he was home and he wanted me to come over and meet someone. I said to myself, I'm not in the mood to be meeting people.

I grabbed my keys from my purse before unlocking my vehicle. I tossed the folder on the passenger side seat with information about the abortion that I would be having the next day. The clinic was required to give us the booklet of info although I didn't want it.

"You're leaving?" Stephanie questioned.

"No, not right now but in a little bit. Ontavious wants me to come down to his house for a minute."

We both were walking to the front door when Harry, the rooster, decided to run toward us flapping his wings. He flew off the ground and pecked Stephanie on the leg. "Ouch!" she yelled and dropped to her knees.

I raised my foot and kicked him in the chest. He fell flat on his back then sprang to his feet and ran back toward me. Stephanie and I both took off running, and he chased us around the car. The next thing I knew she had found a long stick from somewhere and swung at the animal. Harry didn't have no punk in him. He charged toward her. She swung the stick again, but this time it slipped from her hand and ended up far away in the yard. I jumped on top of her car, and she was finally able to hop up there too.

"Aunt Ruby!" I called out as loud as I could, panting and trying to catch my breath.

A few seconds passed after Stephanie hollered. "Aunt Ruby, please come to the door!" She looked over at me. "Why Auntie ain't came to the door yet? She must be watching porn, hell," she joked.

I covered my mouth and laughed. "You're a mess, girl. She's probably taking a nap."

The front door slowly crept open. Meanwhile, Harry paced back and forth like the idiot he was crowing, "Cock-a-doodle-doo."

Auntie stepped out onto the porch in her pink housecoat and slippers. "What the hell is going on out here, and why y'all on top of the hood?" she inquired and let out a loud yawn and stretched her arms.

I pointed at the rooster. "I'm gon' need you to calm him down."

Stephanie broke in, "Auntie, make this crazy bastard go somewhere else. I'm too old to be running and hopping on cars and shit."

I elbow bumped her. "Girl, stop cussing in front of her. You know better," I scolded.

"Look, I'm on top of my car running from this dummy down here on the ground. I ain't tryna watch what I say. I'm a thousand degrees hotter than hell right now," she grumbled and rolled her eyes at me.

I started to go in on her, but I let it go. Now wasn't the time or the place to let her have it.

Auntie laughed by herself because we surely didn't think anything was funny. "Stop, Harry," she ordered. He immediately turned and went in the opposite direction. "Y'all come on inside; he won't bother you no more."

We both leaped from the vehicle. "Whew! That thing is crazier than a loon," I said and giggled a bit behind my remark. It was funny that our big grown asses were scared of a creature so much shorter than we were.

We were racing to the door again, but Harry wasn't done with us yet. He aggressively sprinted our way. Before we could get to the door, he flew up and dug his feet into my back. I felt a hot burning sensation, and I knew he had cut my skin open.

My sister angrily grabbed him before he could take off. His wings flapped. He kicked, screamed, squawked, and protested. She got a hold of his skinny legs, flipped him upside down, and held onto him until he hung there without moving.

There was no more flapping. He didn't make another sound, and I was scared that he might not be alive. "Is he dead?" I lowly asked, half-afraid of what the outcome would be.

"Yes, ma'am, and he got exactly what he deserved," she replied and tossed him in the yard. He was limp as a cooked noodle. I maneuvered over to him, leaned over, and saw that his eyes were wide open and he looked like he was staring at the sky.

"You better get rid of him because if Aunt Ruby finds out you killed her rooster, she is going to have a fit." I glanced over my shoulder at her and stared back at the feathery animal.

She brought her hand to her cheek like she was in a deep thought. "What do you think about burying him?"

"Bury him where?"

"In the woods. She'll never find him down there," she answered.

I suddenly thought of a game plan. I dashed in the house and found Auntie with the television blasted watching *Days Of Our Lives*. Layla was in her swing going back and forth. "I will be back in a little bit. Steph wants to go for a walk in your pasture. She says she hasn't been down there since she was a youngster," I fibbed.

Never turning her head from the TV she responded, "That's fine. Y'all go on."

I left out and met back up with my sister who was holding Harry by his feet, swinging him back and forth.

"Let's go down in the woods. She's in there watching her soap opera, so she ain't thinking 'bout us right now," I let her know and headed off to the shed where she kept all of her tools. I slid open the door, reached in, and grabbed the shovel that was positioned by a weed eater. We took off like a rocket down through the woods, running.

I found a spot far in the pasture beside a pine tree. I used my shoe to mash the soil to see whether it was hard. The dirt was hard as a brick, and I knew that wasn't a good place because it would take us forever and a day to break up that dirt. I moved down further and found some soft ground. I handed Stephanie the shovel and let her dig. Sweat poured from her head as she dug a three to four foot deep hole approximately the size of a box in length and width. She snatched Harry up and tossed him in his eternal home. "Bye, fucka. You messed with the wrong one that time," she said and began to throw dirt on top of him. Once she was finished, we raced back home.

I got another text from Ontavious and decided to run over to his house after saying my goodbyes to Stephanie. I swooped up my daughter and her baby bag. I drove apiece down the road to meet up with Ontavious and see who it was that he wanted me to meet.

I took Layla out of her car seat, and I noticed a car with an out of town tag in the yard. After getting my baby out, I walked to the door and was met with a kiss on the lips by Ontavious. I followed him into the den area where a woman was sitting down sipping from a cup. She appeared to be classy by the way she wore her salt and peppered hair up in a bun. She was neatly dressed, and wore a bead of pearls around her neck. The smell of her candy-scented perfume hit me as soon as I entered the room.

"Mom, this is my girlfriend, Sparkle, that I've been bragging about," he said.

She stood, and we embraced one another. "I haven't seen you in so long," I told her.

She nodded. "You're beautiful and all grown up now."

Blushing, I turned to Ontavious. "She's so sweet and we're going to get along just fine." We all smiled and sat down and I was being re-acquainted with his mom. She told me that her daughter drove them both from Texas so that they could see him. The long drive had Ontavious' sister so tired that she was in the back room napping. The mother and me talked a long time while she held Layla in her arms and played with her.

"Oops, I think somebody has made a stink," Miss Justine announced and handed Layla over to me.

"Gosh. I left her baby bag in the car. Ontavious can you go out to my ride and get it for me, please?" I asked him.

"No problem."

He stepped out and his mom and me continued talking. "I will be a happy woman when my son decides to make a family and give me some grandbabies." She smiled. "Your daughter is so precious and well behaved."

"Yes for the most part she's a sweetheart."

She placed her hand over mine. "Let me say this to you. I love my son more than anything in this world does and he's my everything. You seem to be a sweet young lady and I'm not just saying this because he's my son, but he's a keeper."

Ontavious came back after several minutes without the bag. "Sparkle come here." He curled his finger and left out. I trailed him outside.

"Baby, you must not have looked because the bag is in my ride. You must need some glasses. You may need to give yourself an eye-exam," I teased and was about to open my vehicle. I could see the baby's bag on the seat. I shook my head. "Boy, are you blind?" I asked.

I smiled and looked back at him. He came in closer and removed some papers from under his shirt. "So, you're pregnant?" he asked with a scowl.

Well, I'll be damned. I left the folder under my daughter's bag. Now, I had some serious explaining to do that could cost me my relationship.

Trust Is Everything

Sparkle

I looked like a paused DVD and tried to figure out how I'd get myself out of this one. Damn, I'm slipping, bad. How did I forget that the folder was in my whip under Layla's baby bag? I stood there and didn't know whether I should shit or go blind. Neither one of my choices was realistic, but I was so nervous that I might have considered them.

"Why were you plundering through my shit?" I asked, pretending to be mad and switch the conversation over to his wrongdoing.

"As soon as I lifted the baby's bag, there it was. When were you planning on telling me, Sparkle?" I could tell I had hurt him by the way he stared at me, let out a long sigh, and walked off.

I grabbed him by the arm. "I'm sorry if I hurt you, Ontavious. That wasn't my intention. I got pregnant when I was living in Jackson, and I am sorry. I didn't say anything to you because I didn't want to ruin what we have together. I care about you, and I want to share my future with you," I opened up and said.

"I feel that I can't trust you. If you kept that from me, what other secrets are you hiding?" He snatched his arm away, looked me up and down, and looked away.

"It's not like that. I wasn't trying to complicate our relationship that is why I held it in." I did my best to explain.

"I've worked hard all of my life to get to where I am. I have everything that I could have ever wanted, but the one thing that my life is missing is a woman who knows how to be honest and loyal to her man." I was knocked off my feet that he said that to me. He picked up where he left off. "Women are always complaining that there are no good men out here. I'm a good one and I don't deserve this shit."

I suddenly felt a terrible weight on my shoulders. It was like a giant stone had been placed on me, and I couldn't catch my breath or move. His words cut through my heart. I felt that I had betrayed him, and I could see it in his eyes.

"Baby, I'm sorry. I have been more than loyal to you." I reached for his hand, but he quickly moved it away from me.

"If you were devoted and trustworthy, you wouldn't have hidden anything from me. You're just as bad as my ex-wife with the secrets and the bullshit. You aren't ready to be in a committed relationship. You should have stayed single."

"Are you mad because I'm pregnant, and now you want to break up with me?"

He got all up in my space. "Listen, li'l girl, I'm a grown ass man. I can handle you being pregnant, and I could have accepted that because it happened before me. What I cannot accept is a liar."

I shrugged. "I'm sorry that you feel that way but from what I heard I'm a whole lot better than the last skank that you had. I haven't cheated on you one time. I'm not even interested in any other man, and you want to belittle me and talk stupid like I don't have feelings."

He walked away from me. "Come and get Layla out of the house, and I want you to leave," he demanded.

I was saddened, but I followed his orders.

From Bad To Worse

Stephanie

I stood outside of my apartment placing the key in the keyhole. The sound of the music group, The Commodores', 'Night Shift' and people chattering traveled outside from the inside of my place. I thought to myself," I kno' good and hell well that James ain't got no junkies up in my house." We never had company at our apartment.

I twisted the key to the right and opened the door. Four heroinheads that we dealt with on the streets parlayed in the front room. A married couple named Bertha and Alvin sat on the couch with their heads leaned back. I already knew what was wrong with them; they were high as the sky. James was conversing with a trick bitch named Jess, and they were talking and laughing up a storm. I quickly knew what he had been doing while I was gone.

"All you mothafuckas better get the fuck out of my house!" I snapped, but nobody moved. I slammed the door shut and maneuvered my way into my bedroom. I could tell that somebody had been on the bed. The pillows had been rearranged, the comforter pulled back, and a string of blonde hair was on the top sheet. I took a deep breath and counted to ten before I stormed into the front like an enraged bull.

I snatched Jess up by her blonde weave. "Bitch, you been in my bed?" I questioned her.

James sprung to his feet. "It ain't what you thinking, Steph. We all went in the bedroom. I locked the door, and we shot up."

I tossed my hands in the air. "Are you stupid or something? All you lazy mothafuckas want to do is get high and lay around like some pregnant bitches. You need to go find a job and get off that shit!" I went off. "I hope y'all ain't been in here sharing needles."

James rubbed my arm. "Baby, now you kno' I ain't never used the same needle wit' nobody." He reached in his front shirt pocket, pulled out an insulin syringe, and showed it to me. I looked around the room, and the rest of them had pulled out their syringes and upped theirs to prove to me that they weren't sharing.

The small empty balloons that once had been filled with smack were all over the floor. I was more than fed up. "I want all of you out of my house, and I won't be repeating myself!" I hollered.

The married couple slid off the sofa and slowly walked out. Jess stayed there and pretended that she hadn't heard a word that I had said. She plopped down beside James and watched the television.

I snatched her by the arm. "Bitch, are you deaf or just plain dumb?"

"I ain't neither one. I'm not leaving unless James tells me to leave," she firmly slurred and jerked her arm away from me.

"Well act like it and get the fuck out," I ordered with venom in my voice.

I turned to James and pointed at the trick who seemed to want a good ass whooping. "Are you fucking this hoe? What the fuck is her problem?"

"Steph, she's only an associate. I wish you wouldn't come in here ordering mothafuckas to leave. Don't make me choose between you and my friends."

"I told them to go because I don't want this stuff around me anymore." I re-directed my finger to the empty balloons spread all over the carpet.

Jess broke in, "James, I think it's about time you find a woman who knows how to submit. She's too damn bossy, and you need to put your grown man pants on and act like the man of this goddamn house."

I wasn't going to take anymore of this hoe's smart mouth. I punched her as hard as I could, dead in the mouth. Then, I clenched a handful of her cheap tracks with one hand while popping her with my fist with my other. She was defenseless for a minute until she got the nerve to kick my leg. I grabbed a hold of her legs and drug her to the front door. I kicked her until she finally got up and sprinted outside. When I slammed the door, I was ready to light James up. I suddenly heard banging on the front entrance along with Jess' voice, "James, c'mon, and let's go. You don't have to stay in there with that stupid woman."

He looked at me like I was an enemy. "I guess you done forgot that you ain't always been clean. You didn't have to treat my people like that. I'm gone." He walked out of the door and didn't look back. I was surprised, but I shouldn't have been. He had actually chosen drugs over me, which was confirmation that it was over between us.

The Enemy

Sayveon

After I had dropped Carmen off I went home and relaxed for a minute. I had to leave when Pops hit me up saying that he needed to holla at me and Rich, together.

The world was dark, but the city of Jackson was full of lights stretching for miles. In the sky, I could see a thousand stars and constellations. Then my eyes peeped it. As I drove, I looked in my rearview mirror several times and noticed that a black Ford F-150 with tinted windows followed me. I turned my left signal light on and dipped in front of another car. The strange truck did the same and still ended up on my bumper again. I pressed down on the accelerator and speeded up. The person then gave chase and tried to ram the truck into me to run me off the highway. I grabbed the steering wheel and forced the car to stay on the Interstate.

I reached under my seat, upped my steel, and fired off two rounds. The driver of the truck bust back, shooting at me. I almost ran off the highway for the second time. The vehicle sped and disappeared in the night. I was shook and would be glad when I found out who was behind all of the bullshit.

By the time I ended up at Pops' crib, I was on paranoid. Every day it was some new shit wit' whoever was after me. I had made up my mind that I would definitely keep some heat on me at all times. I wasn't gon' get caught slippin'.

I made it to Pops' crib shortly after, and me and Rich sat down at his kitchen table where he was grubbing. He told us to fix us a plate, and we did. We were there eating mash potatoes and gravy, smothered pork chops, greens, and jalapeno cornbread. To be a man, Pops could cook his ass off.

"Son, I have spoken to you already about my situation with Jackie," he said to me while using his knife and fork to cut up the meat. "I need you two to leave out in the morning headed to Florida. I will give you the address to her mother's house and her home. She's claiming she's down there checking on her mother and trying to sell her house."

Chewing his food and talking at the same time, Rich asked, "So, what you need us to do?"

"I suspect that she is having an affair with someone down there. I only need to know who the person is, and I will deal with the rest." Pops sighed and drank a sip of ice tea. "While you all are down there, I need thirty keys dropped. It's in the same place and location as last time, Sayveon."

"That's cool. I gotchu," I replied.

Rich spoke. "We'll make the drop, but I'm still tripping out on your wifey creeping on you."

"She recently told me that she's expecting a baby. I know that it's not mine because I had myself fixed right after my last daughter was born. I want you two to check up on her and see what's going on. I didn't say a word to her about her being pregnant, and I won't. She'll feel the pain when I bust her." He stopped eating and banged his fist on the table. "She has betrayed me and I won't stop until I find out who she's fucking. I'll dead her and whoever he is."

Rich let out a loud laugh. "C'mon now, Big Al, you kno' that she's younger than you, and ole' girl gon' be letting somebody hit when that fire needs to be put out. I mean, it is what it is. Y'all had been living in two different states for the longest. I'm surprised somebody ain't been knocked her up."

Without cracking a smile, Pops pointed his finger, and I knew that he was pissed off. "Let me tell you something, being loyal has no age limit. I always respected her, although I was married I gave her the life of a queen. I took care of both of my children, and I always had her back. Don't give me that bullshit. She wasn't worried about my age when she spent my money."

There was a brief stillness, and I could feel the anger coming from Pops. He stared Rich down, but Rich continued to eat and didn't make eye contact with Pops. To eliminate the tension, I joined in and changed the subject. "I'll be ready to get on top of this, and I hate that Jackie flipped the script. It's better to kno' than not kno' who the enemy is." I looked around the room. "After I make this run, I think I need to go hibernate and chill for a while. I'm stressed to the max."

Rich nodded. "I feel you. I need one my damn self. Maybe we can get our girls and find somewhere to go. I'm down."

"What about you, Pops? Are you down for a vacation?"

"No, Son. I have too much other shit going on right now." He pulled the lobe of his ear then stroked his chin. "I'm going to call it a night. You two can clean up this mess and lock the door behind you." He excused himself from the table and bounced out to his bedroom.

I hopped up, and me and Rich cleaned up the kitchen, placed the dishes in the dishwasher, and walked to the door. "We out, Pops," I hollered at his bedroom door.

"Goodnight! Your rental car has been booked. The paperwork to pick it up is on the end table as you head out of the door. Take off in the morning and keep me posted." I could tell from his low tone that he was frustrated and exhausted.

Ending It Early

Stephanie

It was two minutes after eight o'clock when I drove into the Olive Garden parking lot in North Jackson. I noticed Marcus parked two spaces over when I was park searching earlier. I turned the car off and placed my metallic silver colored, four inched heeled open- toe Coach pumps on the concrete and stood. I knew I looked sizzling hot in a black frame-hugging mini dress with a diamond encrusted bust line. I tossed my black Coach shoulder bag over my shoulder, closed the door, and proceeded over to his car.

Marcus stepped out of his ride wearing a nice white button up shirt, black slacks, and a pair of black Giorgio Armani shoes. He was looking good and dressed nicely.

"Hey, sexy," he greeted showing his pretty whites.

I blushed before saying, "Hello. How are you?"

"Good now that I see you. You look beautiful."

I felt like telling him that I looked like a unicorn earlier with that small knot in the middle of my forehead. Thank God, I had swooped my bang, and it could no longer be seen. Instead of going through that story with him I simply said, "You're so sweet and thank you."

He grabbed my hand, and we walked inside. The hostess asked, "Will this be a table for two?"

I shook my head and responded, "Yes."

"Follow me," she said. She led us to a back table. We were told that our waitress would come in a minute.

After we were seated, our conversation took off. I loved the way he made me laugh and blush at the same time. I felt attractive, and I was eating up the attention that he was giving. All of it took my mind off the stupidity I had gone through at my place with James and his smackhead friends.

My mind drifted off to what had happened earlier and how he walked out of the door behind Jess. I really couldn't believe how quickly things had changed between us. One minute, he's working and giving me everything that I wanted and needed. The next minute, he's shooting up again and not giving a damn about anyone but himself.

"Where's your mind, Miss?" he questioned holding the menu in his hand.

"I was just thinking that's all."

I began to look over the menu when I heard a friendly voice. "Hi, I'm Mandy. Did I give you all enough time to find something on the menu or should I allow a few more minutes?" It was the young while girl standing there with her small pad and pen in her hand.

"I'd like the Chicken Gnocchi soup. For my entrée I'll take The Three Cheese Pomodoro Ravioli," I told her. "And a glass of lemonade."

She wrote everything down. "Are you ready to place your order, sir?" she asked Marcus who was still browsing through the menu.

He looked up. "Yeah, I'll have Garden Salad, the Shrimp Penne, and a coke."

"I'll be back shortly," she let us know and walked away.

While waiting for our food, we had a talk and tried to get to know one another. He was very interesting, and I loved conversing with him. But the truth was, he was married, so I couldn't get my feelings involved.

"I like the fact that you and I can laugh, and we seem to like the same things. We have a lot in common. I haven't laughed this hard in a long time." He gave me a wink.

"I needed this after the long day that I had."

"Me, too," he admitted. He let out a long sigh and rubbed his forehead. "I am about to go through a divorce. My wife moved out a few days ago, and I received divorce papers in the mail today."

My eyes grew big from the unexpected surprise. "I'm sorry to hear that."

He waved me off. "It's okay. We hadn't been happy in quite some time. It hurts like hell but I've been through way worse in my lifetime."

"We both must be having a crazy day because my ole' man left today. I have a feeling that I won't be letting him come back," I vented.

"Maybe you will."

I ignored his comment and changed the subject because deep down inside I knew that wouldn't be happening. "So, how was work? I know being an attorney has to be fun."

He chuckled before taking a sip of lemonade from his glass in front of him. "It was pretty good. Being an attorney has its good side and bad side like every other job, but it pays well. I've lived a luxurious lifestyle."

"That shit turns me on," I flirted. I gave him a cute smile and giggled.

He returned my smile with his own. We both had started to give the other very intense eye contact before being interrupted by the waiter. Dang, I was disappointed that she disturbed us because my kitty was jumping, and my panties had gotten moist.

"I have your dinner, and I hope you all will enjoy it," she said placing the food on the table. "I'll come back later to check on you all." She turned and walked off.

Marcus said the grace, and I picked up my fork thinking, *I could get used to being around him. I'm enjoying his company.* If everything worked out between us, I could be living good without a care in the world.

Right before we were ready to leave, I got a call on my cell phone from a number I didn't recognize. I picked up after the second ring.

"Hello." I pressed the phone closer to my ear and turned the volume up on the side so that I could hear.

"Is this Stephanie?" a masculine voice wanted to know. His voice was cracking and he sounded nervous.

"Yes. Who's this?"

"This is James' cousin Adrian. He came over here earlier, and now he's in the middle of the floor not moving. I think he's overdosed. I grabbed his phone to call you, but it was dead. So, I called you from mine. When can you come and see about him?"

I couldn't believe my ears. My hand trembled from nervousness, and I began to feel lightheaded. "I will be over there in about thirty minutes. Call the ambulance," I ordered.

"Steph, you been in these streets before. You kno' I can't just call the cops to my crib like that. I ain't tryin' to get in no shit wit' the popo's."

My blood pressure rose, and I placed my hand over my chest. "Look, forget the damn police. You should love your cousin enough to call and get him some help. The paramedics could have been on the way by now."

"Come get him and take him to the emergency room. I told you that I ain't gonna get caught up in nothing."

I sighed. "I'll be there. Does he have a pulse?"

"Hold on." I heard him tell someone to check James' wrist for a heartbeat and see if he had one.

"He has one, but it's not strong," the strange voice told him.

I hung up and immediately told Marcus that I would catch up with him another time. "Is everything okay, sweetheart?" he inquired, placing his arm around my shoulder.

"I have an emergency. I gotta go." I rushed off into the night hoping that James would be okay. I moved in and out of traffic making my way to Canton. James' cousin, Adrian, was a certified junkie. He kept fiends running in and out of his run down house. I said a prayer aloud asking God to have mercy on the father of my two boys. You never know what can happen in a few hours, and all I could do was think back on how he left out of the apartment. I hoped that that wouldn't be the last time that I saw him alive.

Rushing To Rescue

Stephanie

In about twenty- five minutes, I had gotten off the main highway and exited off onto the Canton exit. I pushed through The City of Lights until I made it to Martin Luther King Drive. I passed a few prostitutes and several crackheads hanging out at a corner store on the street. I drove on until I made it to Adrian's half-dilapidated house.

I turned the car off and jumped out. I was so scared that I shivered as though ice had replaced my spine. A cool breeze came through and enveloped my entire body. The walkway leading to the house was cracked, and weeds poked out from them.

I took off and made my way to the door where cobwebs covered the corners. The house should have been torn down years ago.

The door begrudgingly creaked open, and a musty, dank odor crept in my nose. The house was dead silent except for the creaks of the old wooden floor. Black and brown mold dotted the ceiling in big patches, evident of rain seeping through the roof. "James," I called out while looking around for him.

I entered into the dimly lit living room where grime and dirt covered a bookshelf in the corner of the room. It appeared to have been undisturbed for a long time. Wallpaper lay curled on the floor along with a few empty picture frames. I found my way into the hallway, a glimmer of light came from behind the door. I approached the door and pushed it open. Again I called out, "James', where are you, baby?" I had reached the bathroom. The medicine cabinet mirror lay on the tile floor and empty medicine bottles where in the porcelain sink. The only noise in the room was the dripping sound of the faucet. The water was discolored, a brownish concoction.

At the bottom of the tub were a lone mouse and a violent odor made its way to my nostrils. I held my nose. Crusty rags filled the bathtub and cockroaches the size of almonds scurried from under them. I left out of there feeling disgusted from the way the house was kept. I turned to the right, and met my final destination. The door didn't easily open. I pushed it with force. Stepping inside I noticed that Jess was holding James in her arms, rocking him like a baby.

"What the fuck?" came out of my mouth before I knew it. "Did you hear me calling out for him?"

She didn't speak a word instead she ignored me and continued to rock him.

"Bitch, can you hear?" I asked with a frown.

"Everybody that was here left. They got scared and ran off. He barely has a pulse. I think he's dying," she mumbled.

"Did you call an ambulance, or you just in here rocking him like he's yo' nigga?" I dropped to my knees and checked his wrist to see if he was still alive. And he was.

"I didn't call nobody. Adrian told me that you were on your way," she made known as the tears poured from her eyes and down into his face.

James' eyes were closed. White dried crust formed around his mouth. I had a feeling that I had to get him some help fast, and I still wasn't sure if even that would save him. I used my cell in my hand and dialed the paramedics.

"911, what's your emergency?" a deep male voice asked.

"I need an ambulance. I just found my boyfriend on the floor. He needs some medical attention."

"What's wrong with him, ma'am?"

I rubbed the water away with my fingertip that dripped from my eye. "He barely has a heartbeat, and I think he's dying! He's unconscious. I need an ambulance," I revealed.

"Ma'am, give me your location, and I'll send some help," he calmly said.

"I'm on Martin Luther King Drive in Canton. You'll see a red Ford Fusion parked on the side of the street in front of a yellow and green house," I informed.

"Okay, an ambulance is on the way."

"Thank you." I hung up and stood over Jess and James. The anger within me was rising, and I felt like if it weren't for his friends, he'd still be living. He wasn't able to distance himself from the people he was around before he got off of drugs. He'd slipped and now this was the price he was paying.

Jess sat there as if she was in a trance and began humming the spiritual tune, 'Pass Me Not Oh Gentle Savior.'

I grabbed her neck with my left hand and began choking the shit out of her. My phone dropped from my other hand, and I used both of them to try to strangle the life out of her. Her eyes were bulging out of her head. "Bitch, if it wasn't for you, he wouldn't be 'bout to die! I told you to get out of my house, but you still felt the need to act like you're his bitch. Now look!" I let my grip lose and stared at James whose head was now hanging from her lap.

"Get the hell away from me with yo' crazy ass!" she yelped and hopped up from the floor. James' head bounced on the floor and he lay there, helpless.

I swung at Jess and punched her right in the jaw. She slapped me across my face, and that brought out the fool in me. I slammed her into the wall, and it collapsed leaving a huge hole and causing her to fall straight through it and land on her ass. I was just about to give her the business again when I heard a siren approaching. I quickly removed myself from the room and ran to the door where I could see red lights and paramedics getting out of the vehicle.

A young black chick knocked on the door. I opened it and led her and the white guy who worked with her into the room where James was. By then Jess was standing there looking silly after having me go upside her head.

"What's going on with him?" the female asked as she checked his pulse. She opened the huge bag that was on her shoulder and checked his blood pressure. "Go get the stretcher," she said to the other paramedic. He left out.

"I think he's had a drug overdose," I disclosed.

She used her finger to open both of his eyes. "His eyes are constricted and non-reactive." She held up his fingers, and I could see that the tips had turned blue. The other paramedical came back with the stretcher and together they placed him on it. "What hospital does he normally go to?" she asked me.

"Take him to The University Hospital. I'll follow y'all there," I said, walking out behind them.

"Does he take any medications that we need to know about?"

"He's diabetic, and that's all. He uses insulin."

"I'll be sure to document it."

I was halfway out of the door when I heard, "I'm sorry that this happened to him, Stephanie. I'll say a prayer."

I turned around and faced Jess. "Tsk. Bitch, fuck you and yo' damn prayer."

She shrugged and walked away. I stood outside until James was placed in the ambulance and followed them to the hospital. On the highway, I called Sparkle and my two boys. They all promised to come to the hospital to be with me. I was going to need all of the moral support that I could get.

Trying To Save A Soul

Stephanie

I pulled into the garage of The University with my heart racing. I jumped out of my ride and took off toward the ER entrance where the paramedics were taking James out and wheeling him inside. He was taken to the back rapidly. I stood beside the wall trying to calm down before having a seat in the waiting room.

A middle-aged Caucasian nurse came from the back and whispered something to the front desk clerk who pointed at me.

"Excuse me. Are you here with James Alderson?" she asked. Her face was blank, and she showed no expression. She didn't want to give much eye contact and that made me feel that something was terribly wrong.

Think positive, Steph, my mind encouraged. "I am."

She gave me a slight smile. "You can have a seat in the waiting room, and the doctor will come and talk to you shortly." She motioned her finger for me to follow her and led me to a small waiting room where I sat alone and waited.

Minutes had passed when I heard a voice say, "Hi. I'm Doctor Michael Woods. What's your relationship to James Alderson?"

"I'm Stephanie Davis, and I'm the mother of his kids. We actually live together."

"Mister Alderson has had an overdose. Our entire medical staff team worked on him. He's been given CPR, and we've done a lot to try and restart everything in the body. However, all attempts to save him failed. I'm sorry, but he passed in the ER."

I broke down and cried my heart out. He put his hand on my back and patted it. "Please give us a few minutes, and you can come back and view the body. A nurse will come and get you shortly." He walked away, and I sat there shaking and feeling as if this all was a bad dream that I was having. But in reality, it was real.

The nurse from earlier suddenly appeared and escorted me to the room where James was and stepped away to give me time with him. The entire room felt cold, and there was a huge heaviness in the air. I felt disconnected from people, places, and things. It seemed as though I was looking at life through a frosted glass.

I slowly stepped over to the bed, and my heart went out to him. I didn't wish this kind of pain on my worst enemy. I lifted the white sheet from his upper body. His arms had bruises and needle marks all over them. His closed eyes made him look like he was sleeping peacefully. I stood there thinking how things would never be the same again. I had begun feeling lost, alone, and deeply questioning everything in my life.

I rubbed his hand and whispered, "I will always love and admire you. You're the father of my kids and I wish you had of tried to live to see our grandkids. I wanted to grow old with you one day and laugh about all of the good times we shared together. But…now…you're…gone," I groaned.

My head collapsed on his body, and I shed many tears.

I kept wishing that he had changed his life around and completely got off drugs. However, I understood that it took an extraordinary person to fight addiction. Like James, most people were simply ordinary.

A Depressing Night

Sparkle

The room where Stephanie sat on the hospital bed holding James' hand made me very sad. I knew that there was nothing that I could do to help her to get over her grief. I stood against the wall with my head down waiting for the funeral parlor to arrive and get the body. I glanced up once and noticed how peaceful he appeared as if he was only sleeping. The white sheet was pulled up to his neck, and I wondered if he had enough time to ask God for forgiveness and get his heart right before he went to the other side.

Stephanie wasn't the most faithful woman in the world, but she loved him. I could tell that she cared by the way she boo- hooed and rubbed his fingers.

"Sister, I really wish that he had of stopped doing smack," she whimpered, her voice trembled from the hurt she was feeling. She continued, "He lost his job, and things seemed to go downhill for him after that. He worked to take care of the kids, and me and I can respect him for that. He tried to do better but got lost again. I know he loved me, and I wish that I could've saved him. Maybe it's my fault because I should have stopped him from leaving out of the door with his 'so-called' friends yesterday. I should have known that shit was gon' eventually kill him."

Stephanie buried her head in her hands, and rocked back and forth sobbing as she did so. The tears streamed down her face. I made a few steps over to her, rubbed her back, and stroked her hair. "It's not your fault, sis. Don't beat yourself up about it. You didn't do anything wrong. When God is ready to call somebody from this earth, it's nothing that you can do to stop it," I tried to comfort.

Gasping for air, she turned her head and sobbed some more.

"Remember the good times that you shared with him," I said. "Like, do you remember that time when you took him to the doctor because his legs and arms were cut up?" I giggled.

"Yes, how can I forget?" she managed to say and snickered. "The doctor came in the room and asked him how all of that happened to him. He told him that I had kicked him out. The doctor said that he shouldn't let that make him throw himself out of a window."

I laughed. "That's when he told him; no you literally kicked him out of the window."

"Girl, I was so mad with this nigga I tried to kick another hole in his ass. That was right after we moved together in our first apartment back in the days. Boy, you took me way back with that one." She rubbed her hand over her eye and wiped the water away.

Suddenly there were two knocks on the door. A black male peeped his head in. "We're here to get the body."

Stephanie nodded and removed herself from the bed. Another young guy who appeared to be in his twenties followed behind as the two wheeled the stretcher in, covered the body, and transported it out of the room. A deep sadness hovered over us as I held my sister in my arms.

The sound of a squeaky door opening caused my neck to twist in order to see who was there. Both of my nephews stepped in. The older nephew, Jason, was taller and was the spitting image of his dad. Jacob's height was average about 5'9, and he had most of his mom's features. They were both as good looking as brand new hundred dollar bills. Jason's eyes were red as a cherry. He must've been crying because he seemed sad. He gave his mother a hug before he embraced me. "Hey, Auntie Sparkle," he somberly spoke.

"Hey, my big ole' baby," I said back.

Jacob held Stephanie close and gave her a kiss on the cheek before he bear hugged me. "How you doing, Auntie?" he mumbled.

"I'm good. I need to be asking you two that. You all know I'm here if either of y'all need me," I said glancing back and forth between the boys. Although they were taller and much bigger than me I always considered them to be my two big babies. I had been around them since birth and practically helped my parents to raise them when their mother and father went off to prison.

"Thanks," they said in unison.

"I guess the people already came and got Dad," Jacob said after looking over at the empty bed where his father once laid. His hands suddenly covered his face; he slumped over and began wailing. "I'ma miss the hell out of him."

I could feel the pain through each word that he had just spoken. His brother comforted him by placing a hand on his shoulder. He soon settled down, and we all walked out of the door and down the hall after agreeing that we would all spend the night at Stephanie's pad.

As the four of us were leaving the hospital, we moved towards three cracked out looking people. There was a man and two women on each of his side. "Why y'all mothafuckas here?" Stephanie burst out.

"We came to see how he's doing?" the man explained with his hands out like he had done no wrong.

"Alvin, you and yo' wife had a lot of nerve to bring Jess down here with y'all." She faced Jess. "I must not have whooped yo' ass good. You need me to get on you again, huh?" She crossed her arms and stared the woman down. Jacob interceded and pulled his mother away from the situation that was about to get out of control.

"How's he doing?" the man yelled as our family proceeded down the hall.

"Because of you all, he's dead," was Stephanie's reply.

I knew that my sister felt the need to blame somebody for what had happened with James. The truth was, he was a grown man, and nobody put a gun to his head and forced him to shoot up. I hoped that she would soon realize that and face the facts. For now, all we could do was depend on each other for enough strength to get pass all of the hurt that lingered inside all of us by his death.

Moving In Silence

Sayveon

The next morning around seven o'clock, I parked the Beamer in Rich's yard. He and Pops had already gone and copped the rental for us to head to The M-I- Yayo. Pops wished us a safe trip and left. Me and Rich had loaded the whip with the work that we would drop off. Rich slid under the driver's seat. I got on the passenger side, and we hit the slab going every bit of eight miles per hour. The sound of Kendrick Lamar's tune, 'Swimming Pools', flowed from the speakers.

I bobbed my head to the music and happened to glance over my shoulder. I noticed the black Ford truck that had been giving me problems to the right of me. I removed my heater from the waistband of my pants and held my finger on the trigger. I was about to let off some rounds when I noticed that it was an elderly black lady probably in her mid-seventies with gray hair driving looking straight ahead.

"Ay, nigga, what the fuck is you doing?" Rich asked and looked upside my head like I was crazy.

I put the steel back on my waistline. "Man, every since my whip got bombed and then I got run off the road, I been on 'noid. Er' time I see a truck like that one, I get ready to squeeze the trigger. It's a mothafucka 'round here that wanna see me dead. And, we already bodied ole' boy that set me up at the club. So, he's eliminated," I went on to say.

"We need to find him quick and give him his issue before you put a bullet in somebody's grandma's dome." He took a deep breath and let it out before bobbing his head to the beat flooding the speakers.

I scooted down in the seat thinking to myself that whoever had beef wit' me better have the Almighty on his side. Because when we met up again, he'd need God for protection.

Rich hopped off the highway and headed down a familiar street. I sat straight up and asked, "Why we coming down here?"

"I'm 'bout to scoop up my ole' lady. I'm gon' let her chill wit' me in Florida. She's cool people. It's all good."

Before I could reject, he had pulled in Nakia's driveway. Nakia's car was gone, and I was glad 'cause I didn't want to see or talk to her.

LaShune came out of the front door all smiles dressed like she was straight out the gutta. She was wearing a black mini skirt that was so short and tight it looked like she had borrowed it from a kindergartner. She also wore a white baby tee, thin black jacket, and weave that flowed down to her ass. As soon as she made it up the gray pavement and to the two-door car, I got out so she could get on the backseat. "Heyyy, Sayveon," she sang out.

"What it do, shawdy?"

She removed her Louis Vuitton luggage bag from her shoulder, tossed it on the seat in the back, and sat down.

"Heyyy, baby," she said to Rich.

He showed all of his teeth. "What's up, baby doll?" I closed the door and hoped that this trip went by fast, especially with that trick sitting in the back.

Rich jumped back on the highway, and we headed out of town. I held my head back on the headrest thinking about Sparkle and my baby girl, Layla. I knew that I had fucked up too bad to ever get back wit' Sparkle, but it was hittin' a nigga hard in the chest to kno' that another dude was around my seed. Fuck it though. I had to swallow that pill and keep it moving. That was one of the downfalls of separating from my baby's mamas. I didn't want nobody other than myself to raise my girls, but there were some things that I had no control over.

I rubbed my hand over my sleepy eyes and felt a finger moving up and down my back. Then, the strong scent of liquor ran up my nostrils. I turned around and asked, "You sippin'?"

LaShune gave me a wink. "Yep, I'm 'bout to be throwed. You want some?" she asked, pouring Crown Royal in a Styrofoam cup. She upped a coke from her purse and mixed it in with the alcohol.

"I'm straight." *Drunk bird ass bitch!*

"Baby, you want some liquor or some of me?" she asked Rich.

"Some of you, but I'll get that later," he flirted back, like he was proud. Must've made him feel like he had a winner on his team. "I need to stop at the gas station up a little further and get some snacks and drinks for the highway."

He pulled in to a Shell's gas station. "Good. I need to run into the ladies room," she added her statement.

They both got out and went inside. I just chilled. A few minutes went by when LaShune came bouncing out of the store with a pack of gum in her hand and a small brown bag. I got out, pulled the seat up, and let her get back in the car. She moved over further and sat right behind Rich's seat this time.

"Sayveon, stop trying to act all hard like you don't want these lips all over that long dick you got," LaShune flirted. She pulled a chocolate Hershey's bar out of the bag and unwrapped it with her teeth. Her dark brown eyes gleamed with a sense of purpose.

"Rich is my boy, and I ain't tryna cross that line wit' you. Stop sweatin' my dick." I turned back around and shook my head.

"Look."

I looked over my shoulder again. She licked up and down the candy bar before using her two front teeth to bite off a piece, staring into my eyes the whole time. She held a piece of chocolate in her mouth for a few seconds before gently rolling it over and over with her tongue. She pushed a piece of sucked candy out of her mouth and let it rest on her bottom lip. "You wanna taste it?"

"Nah. You need to stop trippin' wit' that bullshit."

She ignored me. Some melted chocolate lay on her lower lip as she ate it; she then licked it off seductively. Her eyes drifted off toward the front of the store. I twisted my neck and noticed that Rich had walked out of the store.

"I'm gon' fuck you," I heard her say.

I pretended not to hear the clown ass bitch and looked out of the window. Rich slithered back under the driver's seat. Ole' girl had a phat ass and was dymed up, but Rich was my boy. I didn't wanna play him like that. But the more I thought about it, she had some fiyah head and if she kept on, my joint would be down her throat touching her tonsils.

A Sudden Call

Sparkle

I was on my way to the clinic the next morning with Stephanie. I had tossed on my gray jogging pants, a big white t-shirt and white tennis shoes. The clinic had informed me to wear loose clothing to have my procedure done, and they told me to be sure to bring a maxi pad. I was afraid and excited to get this shit over with. I patted my leg out of nervousness. I held my head down and then looked over at Stephanie. I made a mental note to pray for her and the boys. I hoped that they would be able to one day recover from the death of James. I knew that Stephanie was mourning, but she still offered to take me to the clinic. That's what I call a strong survivor, and she had shown me that regardless of the past we had, she still loved her little sister.

My cell rang, so I reached down in my purse and pulled it out.

"Hello," I said after seeing Ontavious' number show up on my caller I.D.

"How you doing?" he had the nerve to ask. Before I could respond, he kept on going. "I am upset with the way you handled this whole situation. I'm not against you bringing another man's child into this world. I'm not insecure, and the baby isn't at fault for being conceived." He paused for a minute. "Whatever you decide to do is on you, but I want you to know that I'm here if you need me."

At that moment, I had been shot in the heart with Cupid's arrow. I was a victim of love and felt as though I was about to go into a trance.

"I appreciate your understanding." Before I knew it, I had dropped my guards. "I love you."

"I love you, too," he gently cooed in my ear. We said our goodbyes and ended the conversation.

I sat there thinking, *Dang, I've been blessed with a good man.* "Girl, what's up? You in love over there?" Stephanie wanted to know with a smirk.

"Yes, Ontavious just told me that he'll support whatever choice I make."

"So are you going to keep it?" she curiously questioned with a raised brow.

"I'm not sure. I've gotten confused." I rubbed my temples, wondering what I'd finally do. I had to make up my mind whether I would have it or not. I had a big decision to make.

My Final Decision

Sparkle

The worker at the clinic gave me pills in a small white cup. I tossed them down the back of my throat and swallowed them with the cup of water that the facility provided. My hand shook uncontrollably as I wore the thin white gown. There were about fifteen other young women in the back area with me who also took medication to calm their nerves and was supposed to ease the pain. My basket with my clothes in it stayed beside me. I sat there in the room that was cold as ice shivering and feeling as if I was about to have a panic attack.

A young white chick rose and grabbed her basket full of clothing after her name was called. Her long wretchy hair dropped midway down her back. Her oily skin shined as her big eyes dropped to the floor. She walked into the hallway and off to a room. I could tell she was just as afraid as I was.

"Sparkle Davis," the voice called. I stood, clutched the basket, and dragged myself behind the nurse. She led me into a ghost white room. "I need you to lay back and raise your gown up." I did as she told me and she put my feet up on a steel footrest connected to the board that I was laying down on. "The doctor will soon be in," she assured me.

"Okay," I dryly spoke.

"Are you in school anywhere?" she questioned, making small talk.

"Nope."

There was a knock on the door and a short bald abortionist stepped into the room. "Hello. I'll be performing your procedure today." He sat on the short stool and got in between my legs. "I'm about to inject a local anesthetic to numb the cervix." He waited a minute or two. "I'm going to dilate you, and then I'll clean you out."

I was silent. The nurse stood over me and held my hand. "You're doing well," she encouraged, leaning over staring into my face. All I heard was a vacuum suction. After a 'lil' bit she asked the doctor, "Is something wrong?"

"It's trying to get away. I've tried four different times."

What the fuck did this mothafucka just say? I asked myself.

I was stunned. What he said slapped me in the face and shook me like a ragdoll. I closed my eyes and prayed that God would forgive me and not let me bust hell wide open. I couldn't believe that I was actually doing this.

"It's done," the abortionist ended up saying. He put away all of his tools, wished me a good day, and left out.

The nurse rubbed my arm. "Sweetie, you can put your clothes on. Place the maxi pad in your panties and let me know whether your bleeding is heavy or not. I'll be outside of the door." After she left out, I cried. A part of me died in there along with my child. I knew what I had done was wrong. I had murdered my baby.

Once I had made it to the recovery room, a worker came over and placed a heating pad on my stomach along with a blanket. She checked my blood pressure and told me to relax. An hour went by before I was told I could go. Before I left out the worker went over some paperwork with me. "Here is your detailed sheet of aftercare instructions." She pushed the paper toward me. "We are going to provide you with your medication. You need to take it as instructed on the label." She gave me a big smile and asked, "Are you feeling okay, honey?" She seemed nice but I wasn't in the mood to return the kindness.

The friendly black woman cocked her head to the side, curiously waiting for a response. "Am I going to hell?" It came out without me even thinking of what I was saying.

"No sin is any greater than another in my book." She brushed it off. "You can expect the symptoms of pregnancy to disappear after the third or fourth day. If breast tenderness, queasy stomach, tiredness, and frequent urination persist, do not hesitate to call the clinic. You can reach someone 24-hours a day, seven days a week."

I sighed. "I'm ready to go home. My stomach is cramping me, bad." I held my belly and hoped that the cramps would let up.

She nodded. "I totally understand. Let me further explain your instructions, and then you can go."

"Fine." I licked my lips and frowned.

"For the next two weeks, you will need to take good care of yourself. Get plenty of rest, eat nutritious foods that will help your body heal, and do not engage in any strenuous activity such as sports or heavy lifting. To prevent infection: no swimming, tampons, sex, fingers, or douching. Call if you experience any problems and a nurse will determine whether you need to come in for a visit." She gave a fake ass smile and sent me on my way.

As I walked down the steps with Stephanie to get to her vehicle, my heart felt heavy. I looked into the sky wondering what God thought of me.

Steph had been quiet that day. She merged onto the Interstate and stayed in the right lane. We traveled the speed limit when a black truck decided to ram into the side of Stephanie's car.

I screamed, "Is this mothafucka crazy?"

Stephanie held onto the steering wheel and struggled to keep the automobile in the highway. The automobile crossed into our lane and almost hit us again, which my sister was able to avoid. She blew her horn at it.

I could see him yelling and screaming, although the truck had light tint. He let his window down enough to put his middle finger out of it.

We were about ¼ mile down the highway when he caught up with us again. My adrenaline pumped fast, and I was baffled as to who would be trying to hurt us. This was some bullshit, fa real.

Drama From The Other Side

Stephanie

I had the worse experience of my life when a vehicle attempted to run me and Sparkle off the road. I mashed the gas all the way back to my apartment. I had already lost my kids' father; I didn't want to lose my life as well. I needed to be here for my family.

Once at the apartment, I noticed that my boys' cars were both gone, but it was just my luck that my silly ass mother-in-law's automobile was parked in my parking spot. I hated that bitch with a passion and wasn't in the mood for her. I whipped in right beside her. She posted up in her '12 pine-tree green, four-door Cadillac XTS with her phone in her hand. Her lips moved a mile a minute. Her daughter Atasha, accompanied her. Atasha glanced over at me and rolled her big eyes. That was just like their messy asses to come to my crib unannounced. I would've found another stop to make before returning home had I known that she was here.

Me and Sparkle got out of my car, and that's when all hell broke loose. James' mother, Ms. Glenda Jackson, and her daughter both got out of their vehicle as well. Glenda had her phone in her hand. "Girl, I'm gon' have to call you back. I'm over here with Stephanie now. Let me check this whore, and I'll call you back later on today," she broadcasted to someone on the other end of the line. She hung up and placed her hand on her wide hip looking like Rasputia from the movie *Norbit*. "Look, I came over here to ask you a question. I got a call this morning from somebody saying that you did something to kill James and sent him to the hospital where he died yesterday." This bitch had some real nerve to come over to my crib talking out the side of her neck about a rumor she heard in the streets.

My jaws almost dropped to the floor. "If you don't get the fuck out of my face, I'ma punch you in yo' shit," I threatened with a balled up fist.

"If you lay yo' pinky finger on me, I'm gon' beat yo' ass so bad you'll be the only bitch in heaven in a wheelchair. Now fuck up and hit me," she cautioned, talking with her hands acting ghetto.

I backed up a few steps to try to pour water on the fire that was burning. "You better gon' on before I put a hurting on that ass."

Atasha broke in. "Bitch, don't throw threats at my mama unless you can back that shit up." She played bodyguard and stood by her mammy.

"I'm gon' gone give both of you bitches what you asking for," I said and swung off on the mama with a mean left blow to the eye.

"You got me fucked up!" she screamed.

She clocked me in the head and threw blow after blow at my face. I grabbed her by the collar of her dress, tossed her big fat ass on the hood of my car, and went stupid. I punched her in the face area and then clutched the hem of her short dress before slinging her almost causing her to hit the concreted parking lot. She came back harder and ran into me like a big bull, knocked me down, and dragged me by my hair. "Bitch, let my damn hair go, you big hoe!" She ignored my demand and continued pulling me. She stopped for a few seconds to catch her breath, raised her foot up, and kicked me several times in the mouth. I thought all of my teeth would be knocked out from the force of her kicks.

"Get off my mothafuckin' sister," I heard Sparkle say. The next thing I knew, the elephant went down to the ground with a bang! My sister had pushed her down. We rolled around on the concrete pulling hair, scratching, and hurling insults before I was able to climb to my feet. Wrestling with this big mothafucka was like being in a match with a buffalo. I slammed my shoe down into her belly and tried to stomp a mud hole in her. Her dress flew up and every bit of that cottage cheese looking cellulite showed on her flabby legs and flat ass. Then, she had the nerve to have on a pair of hot pink thongs. Ugh! I damn near went blind.

Ms. Jackson grabbed a hold of my leg and wouldn't let go. I fell on top of her, and that's when I put in my work, banging her dome with my knuckles. "I'm tired. Get off me, I can't breathe," she said between her panting. She breathed hard, sweat dripped from her greasy face.

"I ain't getting off of shit. Fuck you." I spit in her face and snatched her hair until her fake ponytail came out.

I smacked her in the face over and over again with her long weave.

"Gimme my damn hair," she commanded and attempted to grab the hair from my grasp.

I heard some scuffling going on. I turned around and saw Sparkle and Atasha going head up. Sparkle was boxing ole' girl, but Atasha wasn't goin'. She boxed back. I ran over and together my sister and me double-teamed her. I socked her in the nose and got behind her. I then put my arm around her neck. That move knocked her off her balance, and she fell backward. I put my foot on her neck. "Bitch, I ought to kill you." I leaned over, grabbed her by the neck, and choked her until her eyes almost popped out. I finally let her go. I glanced over my shoulder. I noticed Sparkle had walked off and bent over.

Ms. Jackson and her daughter got in their car, and the old hag yelled out of the window while leaving. "Bitches! We ain't through with y'all. You did something to my baby, and you killed him," James' mammy accused, lips so big she needed a kickstand to hold them up. I couldn't stand that heifer, and I was glad she went on 'bout her business.

I made my way over to my sister and placed my hand on the lower part of her back. "Sis, you good?"

She held her stomach with one hand and planted her other on her forehead. It seemed that she was in pain. "I need you to call an ambulance," she said.

"What's wrong?"

"I'm hurting so bad that I think I'm 'bout to die," she admitted. She stood straight up, and I could see large blood spots on the back and seat of her pants. "I'm cramping, and I think I've started to hemorrhage. I feel something warm running down my leg," she managed to whisper as she heavily breathed.

My heart fell to the ground. I couldn't lose my sister; I had already lost James.

Dealing With The Issue

Sparkle

After the paramedics picked me up from Stephanie's apartment and took me to Mississippi Baptist Medical Center, I had a chance to think while waiting in the ER. All I wanted to do was sit there and cry. I wanted to go to the clinic's dumpster and get my baby out. If only I could live this day over again, but my decision to have an abortion was final. I couldn't go back. There were still things that would probably remind me of the procedure in the near future. I would now dread going to the dentist and hear the suction machine. I wondered what the baby would have looked like and how the sound of its laughter would be. Stephanie was by my side sitting in a chair beside where I laid. The doctor ordered several tests for me to take. One was when they stuck a long vaginal speculum into my coochie that hurt like hell. Ugh! The shit women have to go through.

I had to have a talk with God. I slowly crept from where I lay in a hospital gown and knelt on my knees and began a silent prayer.

God please be merciful, wash away my sins, and cleanse me. I recognize my faults, and I am conscious of what I've done. I have sinned against you and have done what you consider evil. Sincerity and truth are what you require. Fill my mind with your wisdom. Remove my sin, and I will be clean. Wash me, and I will be whiter than snow. Create a pure heart in me and a loyal spirit. Do not banish me from your presence. Give me the joy that comes from salvation and make me willing to obey you. Spare my life and save me, and I will gladly seek your righteousness. I ask this prayer in Jesus' name.

Amen.

Steph came over and grabbed me under the arm. She helped me back into bed.

There was a knock at the door and a short Vietnamese nurse came into the room. "Ms. Davee, thee doctor want me to give you thee two pills. One is to control your bleeding and the otter is to help with thee cramping that you having," she spoke in broken English. She handed me a small white cup and water. I took the orange and white pill out, put them in my mouth, and drank the water. "If you want to stop cramping, I can show you a trick."

I looked up at her. "What is it? I'm willing to try anything so it can quit."

She finger motioned for Stephanie to come over. "Massage her abdomen. Push down starting from below her belly button towards thee pubic hair. Thee rubbing will help to pass blood clot that might be causing some of her cramping. She may also be hurting from some muscle strain and she get more relief by resting." Although her English wasn't up to part, I could understand her, and she was sweet.

Stephanie rubbed down my abdomen in a clockwise direction. She did it about five minutes with the supervision of the nurse and the pain soon eased up.

"Thee doctor want you rest for at least a hour. I'll be at the nurses station if you need me," she stated before leaving out.

"Thank you," I told her.

Stephanie held my hand. "I love you li'l sister."

I chuckled. "I love you too, girl, but the next time you get ready to go to war with an Amazon looking bitch; warn me."

She giggled. "I know right?"

I closed my eyes and drifted off to la-la land. The two pills had me sleepy and high as a Georgia pine.

My Homies Girl

Sayveon

Damn, I was hyped to be in Florida again. It had been a long trip. Rich whipped into the parking lot of Pops' condominium, and we all got out. The sun was shining. I could easily get used to the peaceful sounds of the waves and shorebirds. I could chill to the warm rays of the Florida sun. The palm trees swayed when a relaxing breeze came through and blew my stress away. I felt delivered from all the bullshit that was goin' down in 'The Sipp.' From where I stood, I could see the sandy white beach and couples walking and holding hands while walking barefoot. This place would be the perfect retreat. I was ready to say deuces to the cares of the world.

VIP came out and grabbed LaShune's luggage along with the small bags we had on the backseat while we made our way up to the crib. I grabbed the key from the front pocket of my jeans and opened the door.

VIP unloaded our luggage on the front room floor and he was about to walk out. "Hol' up, partna," I said putting up my pointer finger. I grabbed my loot from the other pocket and peeled him off a fifty-dollar bill. "Good lookin' out."

He nodded. "Thank you, Mister." I closed the door behind him.

"I'm 'bout to go to the store and get some Cigarillos. That long drive got me wanting to get blunted out," Rich said and looked at LaShune. "Let's bounce, babygirl."

"Baby, I'm tired and still feeling a li'l buzzed. Show me where we gon' be sleeping, and I'll just go lay down," she whined.

"I'm 'bout to hit the shower and then get some shut eye til we go handle that business," I said to Rich referring to dropping off the birds in the trunk.

He clutched LaShune's luggage from the floor and led her into the back where they would crash. I stepped over to the fridge, pulled out bottled water, and was gulping when Rich came through. "I'll be right back, homie."

"That's wassup."

I gathered my shit and swaggered into the room where I would rest my head. Pops stayed on some real boss shit by the way he kept the condo set up. There was a king-sized plush bed, large private bathroom with marbled floors, 32-inch flat screen with DVD player, and a view of the ocean. I tossed the luggage on the bed, got my changing gear together, and headed to the bathroom.

I undressed and then grabbed a towel from the small closet. I rubbed my hand over my face and stepped into the shower. I happened to look down at my long, thick wood. "Goddamn, I see why these hoes be jocking a nigga," I said lowly with a smile. I turned on the water and waited for it to get warm. I put the showerhead on my body and let it wet every inch of me. I grabbed the soap and lathered the washcloth. I then began washing my frame.

The shower glass slid back and there LaShune stood, naked as the day she was born. Her gaze quickly went from my eyes and landed on my dick. I ain't gon' lie, shawdy was looking damn good. "Whatchu doin'? Rich gon' kick his foot off in yo' ass if he catches you up in here," I warned, steady eyeing her up and down. She hopped in the shower and never commented on what I had just said. She handed me a condom from her hand and dropped to her knees. My pole got hard as a brick as I rolled the rubber up it.

I let LaShune take over as she sucked me hotly and wetly. She sucked all over my nuts too. I caressed and massaged her titties while she had me in her mouth. My fingers rubbed her sweet pussy with my arms reaching over her back. My fingers slipped inside of her hot tightness. I knelt behind her as she arched her back as sexily as a real bitch would and lifted her round firmly shaped ass in the air. I slid my dickhead up and down her wet folds while teasing her for a long time.

"Gimme that dick, baby," she purred.

I needed no further encouragement. I slid my long, thick hardness just inside her shaved pink lips. The lips surrounding her hole opened like a wet flower in bloom. I dug further inside her slick hot tight walls. This bitch's pussy was fiyah! I held and rubbed her all over as I fucked her hard and deep. I had to hit her spot 'cause she started to grind faster against my dick and kept up with my rhythm. I remained still as she pumped vigorously at her own pace. She moved back against me harder and harder rubbing her clit. My body slapped back against her cheeks firmly and noisily.

"I'm 'bout to come for you, Sayveon. I feel it," she told me with her head held back as she sucked her bottom lip.

She bust off soon after that. She moved back until I sprayed. I leaned over panting 'cause she had me weak as a mothafucka! That's why Rich was so gon' in the head. That pussy was A-1.

There were about four knocks at the bathroom door. "Sayveon, you seen LaShune?" Rich wanted to know.

LaShune's mouth opened wide, and she looked scared as hell. Now, this hoe had me in some straight bullshit. How the fuck was I gon' get this bitch up out of here?

Wrong Place At The Wrong Time

Stephanie

Sparkle checked out of the hospital later on that evening, and I was happy that she was okay. It was the doctor's orders that she got plenty of bed rest. On the way back to my apartment to let Sparkle get her car, my cell rang. I looked down on my lap where it laid and answered.

"Hey, Grandma Annie," I greeted James' grandmother who I loved dearly. Unlike the mammy, we always got along because of her sweetness and kind heart.

"Hey, baby," she softly spoke.

"How you doing?"

"I do pretty good. Been having pains up and down my legs but for a old woman I think I'm doing just fine." She switched subjects. "I heard a li'l 'bout what happened between you and my daughter."

"Um, I'm sorry but she..."

Before I could finish she stopped me in midsentence. "Don't explain anything to me. I know how she can get out and show her behind. Right now, y'all need to get along for the grandkids sake. I really want to see you soon. I miss your company."

"What are you doing right now?" I asked her and looked at the radio clock on the dashboard. It was a little after seven o'clock.

"I'm not doing a thing. You want to come over and hang out wit' this eighty- year old lady?"

"I sure will. Let me drop my sister off, and I'm headed that way."

"See you in a li'l bit, darling." We said our good-byes and hung up.

I made it into the parking zone of Shady Oaks Assisted Living Home in about ten minutes. I parked, got out, and strolled to the front entrance. I entered the elevator along with three other elderly black men. One was in a wheelchair wearing an afro. The tallest of the three favored Bill Cosby. He started to look at me. "You're a pretty gal," he complimented.

I smiled. "That's mighty sweet of you to say."

The older man in the wheelchair asked the tallest one, "Say, Nate, how was your vacation last week? One of the workers told me that you visited California with one of your daughters."

Nate chuckled a bit. "It was supposed to be a getaway trip for me, but my energy ran out faster than my money did." All of the men laughed.

"Tell me about it. Everything on my body hurts and what doesn't hurt---doesn't work," the man in the chair said. He flipped topics. "I don't know where the hell my glasses can be. I searched my room for an hour and still couldn't find them." He opened his shirt pocket like he was trying to see if they were in there.

I snickered. "Your glasses are on top of your head."

He ran his hand over his head. "Well, I'll be damned. Thank-you."

When the elevator made it to the third floor, I started to walk off when I felt a pinch on my ass. I turned around, and the guy in the wheelchair had the nerve to wink his eye at me. "You got a soft one," he said. He grinned and didn't have not one tooth in the front. I grabbed his hand and popped it twice as if he was a little child. "You kno' better," I fussed.

"She whooped yo' ass like you're a toddler," Nate kidded.

I took off and found my way to Grandma Annie's apartment. I knocked a few times. "C'mon in, it's open," she said. She sat on the couch. Her caramel skin was as smooth as porcelain. She had the most cheerful personality and was slightly overweight. Her graying hair was in a bun. The thick framed glasses on her face hung from a chain. She wore a long old-fashioned deep purple dress while knitting.

I leaned over and gave her a hug. She asked for some sugar and put a wet one on my jaw. The older people in The South called a kiss, 'sugar' and would give you a smack on the cheek. That was their way of showing you nothing but love.

"I was just sitting up here thinking how the times have changed," she voiced. "You and Glenda showed out bad today. I heard it through the grapevine, and it disappointed me. She is older than you and she should have known better." She looked up from what she was knitting for a brief moment. "You know about the civil rights movement, don't you?"

"Yes, ma'am. I do."

"What's the difference between the civil rights movement and what's happening in the world today?"

Baffled I answered, "I don't really know except that blacks can use the bathroom wherever whites can. We can vote, and we have the same opportunities as white people." I crossed my leg and placed my handbag beside me.

"All of that is true but the main difference is instead of us fighting against whites, we fight against each other. Women in my day would stick together, and we knew what it was to be a woman and how to conduct ourselves in public. Now, y'all battle it out anywhere and no longer have self-respect. People don't support one another and help the other anymore. There was an old saying that said it takes a village to raise a child. Now there are single women trying to raise boys into men." She shook her head. "Everything has changed."

"Ms. Annie, you're right. I didn't intend on fighting Ms. Glenda, but she accused me of killing

James. I couldn't take any more of her mess," I said, feeling guilty about my behavior.

She held her hand up. "Baby, that's when you should have walked away. Walking away doesn't make you a coward; it makes you the better person. No matter what people may say or call you, you had enough courage to go the other way. That's called making a wise decision," she preached. "I remember Martin Luther King, Jr., Rosa Parks, Malcolm X, Medgar Evers, Thurgood Marshall, Ruby Bridges, Fannie Lou Hamer, and W. E. B. Dubois who all fought for us to be treated equal. Several lost their lives so that we could have freedom. Is that how you want to repay them by clowning like a circus animal?"

I dropped my head in shame. "No."

"Make the older generation proud when we see you going down the street acting classy." She pointed at herself. "Make me smile when I look at you and see a young woman who has the same rights as the white woman standing next to her. Make me happy to say that I fought for civil rights and was a member of the NAACP. I went to jail and was beaten trying to stand up for me and for you." I saw a tear trickle down her face, I could feel her pain, and I got her point.

The door suddenly opened. "That's my boyfriend probably," she said with a smile on her face.

Shocked I said, "What are you doing with a boyfriend?"

She laughed. "I'm old not dead."

In came the elderly man, Nate, who was in the elevator with me. "Hey baby," he greeted her.

Now, ain't this some shit, I thought to myself.

"Hey, honey," she spoke back. He brought himself over and gave her a kiss on the lips. I felt like puking all in my lap. Grandma Annie was too old to be trying to date somebody. Nevertheless, if it made her happy, I'd have to accept it. She looked at him. "Honey, can you get me a dish of ice-cream and why don't you write it down so that you don't forget it?"

He brushed her off. "Tsk, I can remember to get icecream that's simple. Your memory hasn't been the best lately. You may need to jot it down," he kidded.

"Well," said Grandma Annie. "Put some strawberries and whip cream on top. Now, you really better make a note of that so that you won't forget."

"Don't talk silly. A dish of ice cream, strawberries, and whip cream. I won't forget that. My Alzheimer's ain't all that bad." And with that said he walked away and closed the kitchen door behind him. We could hear him getting out pots and pans, and making some noise inconsistent to his preparing a dish of ice cream with strawberries and whip cream on top. Fifteen minutes later, he emerged from the kitchen. He came over to her and gave her a grilled ham and cheese sandwich.

Grandma Annie took one glance at the plate and glanced up at him. "Hey, where are the chips?"

He twisted his body and went back into the kitchen area. "A man ain't worth shit, young or old," she whispered to me. "They wouldn't remember to put their head on if it wasn't already connected to their bodies. Now, I told him ice-cream and this fool comes back with a sandwich."

I laughed and gave her a goodbye hug. "I'll see you later. I love you. I'll let you enjoy your company."

"You better come back to see me," she bossed and tightly hugged my neck.

"You know I will."

I walked away promising myself that I would start conducting myself like a woman. The talk that she had with me really made sense, but I had no idea that the next altercation I encountered would be severe. I could only control my actions. I would soon find out that some situations could quickly get out of hand, and there's no turning back.

Duckin' and Dodging

Sayveon

There I stood wit' LaShune in the bathroom after I had smashed her. She was so shook that her bottom lip quivered. This bitch was 'bout to start a whole lot of bullshit if Rich caught me in there with his girl. He waited for my response on if I'd seen LaShune. "She said something 'bout goin' for a walk on the beach earlier. I think she dipped outside for a bit," I fibbed. I mean, it wasn't like I could tell the nigga I had just banged his hoe's back out.

"Aight, I'ma go check outside and see if she out there anywhere." I heard the front door slam. LaShune peeped out of the door to be sure the coast was clear and struck out of there like a streak of lightning. I jumped into my lounging gear and went outside to see where Rich was and keep him distracted til' she put her clothes on.

"Bruh, she can't be that far," I said to him, pretending to be lookin' for the broad.

"I'm 'bout to see if I can find her out here somewhere." He took off toward the beach area and so did I. I went in the opposite direction; I needed a piece of mind. As I walked along the beach, I noticed that the sun was beginning to set and the ocean's big blue waves crashed against the oversized rocks. The seagulls joyfully flew around in circles in the sky. I closed my eyes for a minute enjoying the peace. I hadn't realized how stressed I was until I inhaled the crisp air that a breeze brought along.

I walked in my red short pants, shirtless enjoying the view. There was a beautiful Chinese and Caucasian looking chick to my right laying down tanning. She looked about 5'3, tiny waist, nice breasts that looked to be a DD- cup, silky smooth legs, long jet- black silky hair, strong cheekbones with medium sized plump lips, and a small pointy nose. Her body was blazing, and I'd most def hit that. She held a book up. Her eyes darted from line to line. She seemed to be wrapped up in her own universe. I swaggered up to her. "What up, ma?"

She glanced up. "Hi."

"You from around here?" I asked, trying to spark a conversation.

"Yes, a matter of fact I am. What about you?" she questioned with a sweet smile that could warm the coldest heart.

"Nah. I'm here visiting. I'm sorry for interrupting your reading."

She shook her head saying, "Oh, no you're good. This book isn't all that interesting. I was just trying to read something to pass the time while I'm getting a tan. I think I've gotten a pretty good one. I have been here for a good while." She looked over her toned sexy legs. "So, what's your name, and where are you from?"

"Sayveon. I'm from Mississippi, and what's your name?" I sat down on the sand next to her and hoped that shit didn't find its way inside my pants and irritate my dick and nuts.

"I'm Jia. I've never been to Mississippi before but I've heard you all have really hot weather in the summer. Isn't that where the movie a 'Time To Kill' took place?" she curiously wanted to know.

"Yep. They filmed that in Canton, Mississippi. You don't look like the type to have watched that."

She raised her brow. "I had to do a paper on it back in high school for Black History Month. It was very interesting, and I learned a lot from it. I even made an A on my report."

"Where do you live? If you don't mind me asking?"

"Actually, I live in a condo right in the front."

"Fa real? That's where I'm chilling. I'm in the first building."

"That's a coincidence. I'm in the condo two buildings down from you."

I heard my name being called and turned around and saw LaShune and Rich holding hands walking along the beach. I just finished blazing that broad's pussy, and there she was booed up wit' her nigga. "I found her," he told me.

"Where was she?" I wanted to see what lie she had told.

LaShune chimed in. "I was across the street looking around in the antique shop. When he came back in, I had just gotten back."

"That's wassup," I said.

"We been walking a li'l bit now I'm gon' go back in and watch some TV. When you finish choppin' it up wit' yo' friend, come holla at me so we can handle that business," Rich said.

"Aight." They turned and walked back toward the condo.

I talked with Jia a while longer, got her digits, and promised her that I would hit her up and take her out that night. She had told me that her family owned five Chinese restaurants in Miami, her mother was Chinese, and her father was Caucasian. I would be sure to call her 'cause I could picture myself beating that pussy up.

The Last Date

Stephanie

On my way out of the assisted living home, my cell rang. I snatched it from my purse and saw Marcus' name show up across the screen.

"What's up?" I answered, happy that he had called.

"I haven't heard from you. Is everything okay?" he asked.

"No, not really. James, my kid's dad, died and I've just been going through some things," I said, feeling sad after having to explain why he hadn't talked to me.

He was silent for a li'l minute. "I'm sorry to hear that. I was just about to cook some dinner and invite you over, but I totally understand if you don't feel up to it."

"After the day that I had, I would love to come over. I think it would help to keep my mind off of everything that's going on around me."

"Good." He gave me his address, which was in Byram, Mississippi. I planned to relax at his crib and clear my mind. I had been through enough craziness lately, and I had started to think that it would never end. I needed to unwind. I turned on the radio and my CD played. Listening to Mariah Carey and Miguel's new tune, 'Beautiful' soothed my ears and lifted my spirit.

I used my GPS to find Marcus' house and made it in about twenty- minutes. Even though it was night by now, I could still see his country home. Pole lights surrounded it. He lived in a super nice two story home with a two-car garage. He must've known I was outside because one of the front porch lights came on that shined right on my car. I removed myself from the vehicle and sashayed up to the door. I was about to knock when the door came open and the smell of fried chicken hit me in the nose.

"Hey, beautiful, come inside," he greeted and embraced me with a tight hug.

The inside of his crib looked gorgeous. A formal dining room was to my left. The living room area where I stood had a stone fireplace and cherry wood flooring. A nice sized flat screen television mounted on the wall, had to be at least a fifty inches. The black leather sofa and loveseat brought the entire room out along with the expensive looking pictures on the wall. I sat on the couch. "Your house is really nice," I complimented.

"Thanks. You can sit here or keep me company in the kitchen."

I stood and followed him into the kitchen. I sat down on a stool and admired the granite countertop. "So, what are we having for dinner?" I really didn't have much of an appetite but since he was so nice about cooking I decided that I would at least try to eat.

"Fried chicken, mashed potatoes and gravy, corn on the cob, green beans, and fresh rolls. Does that sound good?" he asked, using a fork to turn over the chicken in the skillet.

We talked and laughed until the food was ready. Then, we had dinner in the dining room. The food was delicious. I ate as much as I could, and he understood that I really didn't have a appetite. I helped him clean the kitchen and after that, we watched TV in his bedroom. He held me in his arms until I drifted off to sleep while he watched a movie. When I did wake up I noticed that the television was off and only a small night lamp beside the bed was on. *Dang, I didn't think I was that tired,* I said to myself and dozed off again.

I was sound asleep when I heard a loud thump outside of the bedroom door. Half awake and nearly paralyzed with fear, I heard footsteps nearing. With my heart pumping, I hid under the cover. "Mothafucka, how you gon' be in here wit' another bitch, and you just fucked me earlier?!!"

I moved the comforter from my face, and Marcus jumped out of bed. The brown-skinned female standing in the doorway scared the hell out of me. I didn't know whether I shoulda been afraid of the gun she was pointing at Marcus or her face. She was at least six feet tall wearing a long sleeved green top and matching pants. She had buckteeth, thin lips, a unibrow, and her eyes spread far apart. *Did he really stick his dick off in this bitch?!!* I asked myself. I wouldn't have touched her with a shitty stick.

"Ashley, what are you doing here?" he calmly asked.

"Something told me you've been cheating and up to no good. You didn't answer your phone none tonight. I knew you were up to some bullshit," she snapped. She held the weapon in her hand while aiming it right at the bastard's head.

I was heated 'cause this negro had me in the middle of him and this stupid bitches mess. If she didn't kill him, I would beat his ass so bad when this was over that he'd wish he was dead.

"This is only a friend. Her kid's father died yesterday, and she needed some emotional support. Nothing went on between us, I promise," he tried to convince. He walked up closer to her.

"If you come one more step, I'll kill you. All you ever did while we were together was cheat on me. You think this bitch is prettier than me, don't you?" Her eyes glanced over at me and quickly landed back on him.

"Baby, I told you the truth. I've never laid a hand on this woman before. I don't know whether she's a woman or a man." He flat out lied.

"Have y'all ever fucked?" she asked me.

Was this trick serious? Like I would actually admit to that when she was standing there with a gun cocked and ready to fire. Hmph, I think not! My answer, "No, we're only friends."

She hesitated and said, "I don't believe you."

She squeezed the trigger and all I remembered hearing was a loud bang. I kept thinking this was a dream until I felt something touch my body. All I could do was hope that I'd be able to see my family again. My boys had already lost one parent, I didn't want them to have to bury me next.

Check Me Out

Sayveon

I came back in the condo and smelled Kush smoke and noticed half of a blunt was in the ashtray in the living room. Rich had fired up before he went in the back somewhere. I didn't kno' where him and LaShune were, but I figured he should have been ready to bounce.

"Oooh, shit this big dick is good, Daddy," I heard LaShune say out loud between her moans. I shook my head. The bitch had just got through letting me hit it earlier. Now, she was back there giving Rich some pussy. Boy, a hoe sho' gon' be a hoe, but she wasn't my bitch. Therefore, I didn't trip it. Rich should have had enough game to know that he couldn't put cuffs on a rat bitch, but he couldn't see nothing 'cause he was blinded by the pussy.

"Damn, this shit hot," Rich told her.

I turned the living room stereo on to drown them out. I went to my room and got dressed in a swagged up fit. I checked myself out in the mirror attached to the dresser geared in a dressy black button up Burberry shirt, black slacks, and some black Belvedere Crocodile shoes. Then, I pulled out the bling. Ballers were notorious for rockin' iced out chains, but I took my flossing to a whole 'nother level. Some settle for the more subtle. There are chosen few who take diamonds and platinum over the top. I was *that* nigga. Around my neck, I hung two gold and 'plat' chains that dangled down to my six-pack. I put on a diamond embroidered rollie watch. Two yellow-diamond pinky rings iced out both of my pinky fingers, and the blinged out three- carat diamonds in my ear had me shining like a celebrity. I looked 'stupid fresh.' I sprayed on a scent by Versace called, Dreamer and waited for Rich.

Thirty minutes had gone by when Rich stepped into the front room where I was phone kickin' it with my new arm candy, Jia.

"What did you want to do tonight?" she asked, sounding like an innocent schoolgirl.

"I'm 'bout to bounce in a few. I'ma let you tell me where you wanna go. It's on you, babydoll."

"You ever been to a strip club in Florida?" she asked catching me off guard. *I knew she was a freak,* I thought.

"Nope, only clubbin'. You wanna go and kick back in one?"

"I've always wanted to go, but I've never been before. Sure, I'm game," she said followed by a giggle.

"Aight, I'll hit you up as soon as I get back."

"Great."

"Be easy," I said before I ended the call.

"Damn, nigga, you done got fly on me," Rich told me after seeing what I had on.

"I'm gon' chill wit' ole' girl that I was talking to earlier. Thinkin' 'bout hittin' the strip club wit' her later on."

"I was gon' take my girl out tonight when we got back. She wanna go site seeing, but I could hit the club wit' you if it's aight."

"I'm aight wit' it. Ain't yo' girl gon' be mad if you leave her?" I wanted to know.

"She's going too. Y'all can just drop us back off at the crib early if y'all wanted to leave there and do something together."

"Bet."

We were 'bout to walk out of the door when Rich yelled over his shoulder, "Baby, I'm gone. Have some clothes on when I get back."

I slithered behind the driver's seat of the whip and texted Pops' people and told him that I was headed to make the drop. He text right back and let me know that everything was good, and he'd meet me there.

I rolled out bumpin' Wale's tune, 'Bad.' I got on the highway and drove about two miles, where the drop off spot was. I parked, popped the trunk and two Cubans who waited for our arrival cleared the birds out, and loaded them to the maroon tractor-trailer that waited beside us. The eighteen-wheeler headed for Louisiana. The shorter cat handed me a duffle bag full of dough. "Here you go, Sayveon.

Gracious," he spoke thanking me. I had dealt with him several times so we were familiar with one another.

"Le invitamos," I spoke in Spanish saying 'you're welcome.' I had picked up on some of the language from Pops. I unzipped the bag, peered inside, tossed up the deuces, and we pushed off.

"If you aight with it, see if ole' girl will give you a few more minutes before we go to the club. I need to shower real quick before we roll off," Rich uttered.

"Gon' 'head and do it. She's on my time," I said in a cocky kind of way. It didn't matter that he wanted to do that. I had to go back in the condo and put the duffle bag in a secure place until we went back home.

It didn't take long for Rich to shower, and he stepped out of the back holding hands with LaShune. In LaShune's free hand, she was holding a cup and more than likely it was full of that liquor. She was forever tryna get wasted. LaShune had on a red mini-dress with some silver peeptoe pumps along with silver accessories. Rich was geared in a crisp gray button down Coogi, black Levi jeans and a pair of black& gray MJ's.

I had called Jia and told her to come to the condo so we could go. It wasn't that much longer that I heard the doorbell ring, and I opened it. Jia stood looking like a fashion model in a fitted black mini skirt, off the shoulder leopard print shirt, and six-inch leopard printed stilettos. LaShune looked tight, but Jia was stylin' on her.

"Jia, this is Rich and his girl, LaShune," I introduced. "They gon' go wit' us."

"Nice to meet you two," Jia spoke.

Rich said what's up but LaShune half spoke with an attitude. She was hatin' on her 'cause she was beautiful. *I'm on one!*

We bailed from the condo in the Challenger with the chicks on the backseat and hit I-95 and ended up at King Of Diamonds. The parking lot was full of flavored whips and the line was from here to Texas. I pulled in and a dude who worked there asked me, "You wanna park close to the door for twenty dollars?"

"That's cool." The door looked to be at least a mile away at this point, maybe further. I opted to park up close. I was 'bout to go in my pocket for the bread, but Rich handed it to me before I could get to mine. I took it from him and gave it to dude. "Good lookin' out," I told Rich.

We all got out, made our way to the long line, and waited until we made it up front. There was a male and female security guard that patted us down real good, checking for weapons. The guard told me that it was twenty dollars to get in. I reached in my pocket, pulled out a big bankroll, and peeled off a c-note. I told her, "I got my peeps wit' me. I'm paying fo' all of us."

I caught Jia eyeing down the guap that I had pulled out, but she didn't come off as thirsty. She had told me that her family owned their own businesses, so I was sure that she wasn't hurting for no loot. I guess she was slightly impressed that I had come out of my pocket wit' a wad of green.

The security guard said, "How many are you paying for?"

"Four."

She handed me my change, a twenty. "Y'all can go on in."

The loud sound of the music screamed in our ears. 'Bandz A Make Her Dance,' by Juicy J. was playing when we stepped inside. The place was huge and looked to be every bit of fifty-thousand square feet with two bars, three areas for V.I.P., photo booth, and a canteen area to order food. The three of us sat down in front of the stage, but LaShune spotted a bar and told Rich she'd find him later on after she, 'got her drank on,' in her words.

I chilled out and watched the two naked stripper's twerk. Wasn't none of that top only shit. These hoes was butt naked dancing together and had some pretty faces, thick hips, and ass for days. Then all of a sudden, the music stopped.

"Thank y'all for coming out. The next performer is Black Velvet. I promise y'all this show is the shit! Hands down! This chick 'bout to turn up," the DJ bragged, from upstairs where he DJ'd.

The stage cleared and a chocolate Ebony Queen showed up on the scene in a black bikini outfit and a pair of black peep toe pumps. Her long wavy black hair flowed down to her ass that was phat to death! The tune of Luck, 'Pole In My Pants,' came on and a spotlight was placed on her. She rubbed her titties while dancing seductively and eased her bikini bottoms off. She did a split and bounced her pussy up and down on stage. She stood and twirled around the pole that was double the length of an average one, looking sexy. A chair was beside her with a wine bottle on top, and she came over and hovered her pussy over the bottle. Slowly the top of the wine bottle went up her hole.

The crowd tossed racks at her and a bunch of niggas, including Jia, stood applauding her. She gradually came back up holding the bottle with her pussyhole. She walked around with it stuck up her. The dudes up front were goin' crazy, me and Rich tossed hunnid dollar bills on stage along with the other ballers who made it rain on her.

Black Velvet squatted down while holding the wine bottle spread eagle. Slowly the bottle came down until it reached the tip. She held it there. She stood and pranced all over the stage, holding the tip of the bottle with her coochie.

"Goddamn, baby, you got some pussy control!" I yelled out.

Towards the end, a bouncer lit a cigarette and held it low enough for Black Velvet to grab it wit' her kitty lips and the broad made her pussy smoke it. When she finished her performance, she got a standing ovation. The sweep up guy picked up all of her money for her while she walked off stage.

LaShune found us and plopped down in a seat right between me and Rich. I could smell the strong liquor on her breath when she opened her big mouth and said to Rich, "Baby, I bet yo' dick done got hard and long as my arm off these strippers."

"But I'm going back wit' you. I'ma knock the bottom out when we get back." He kissed her on the jaw. Nigga was over there cupcakin' a pigeon. I redirected my attention to the entertainment.

"That was some rare shit that she just did. Y'all niggaz, including me, be 'round here talking 'bout we got big dick's," the DJ said and let out a loud laugh. "I couldn't do shit with her; she'd make me feel like I gotta teenie weenie wee-wee. She'd fuck up my ego," he joked. "Thank y'all for coming out to King Of Diamonds, showing love. Get those dead presidents ready because next up we have the always sexy and red dancer, Red Bottom coming out. Don't forget about our tasty food section where they're ready to feed your stomachs. Right now, this performer is 'bout to feed your eyes. Once again, Red Bottom!"

He turned up the music and 'Dance Like A Stripper,' by M. E flowed through the air. Red Bottom was a redbone who showed up wearing a red see through mini dress, red g-strings under it, and red seven-inch stilettos. Her long curly red hair dangled halfway down her back. She slowly danced and took all of her clothes off. Her nice D cup tits were exposed. She bent over and made that ass jiggle. She went over to the pole, climbed up it, spread her legs wide, and slid her pussy down the pole until she landed back on the floor. She crawled across the stage until she got to the center. She did a headstand with her legs spread apart and clapped her ass cheeks. Jia tossed dollars at the stripper. "You're working it, Red Bottom," she egged the dancer on. She wasn't the only one feeling the dyme-piece. Loose money fluttered to the floor, coming from everywhere, accumulating like puddles in a rainstorm. There were so many bills surrounding her that the floor host dressed in black slacks, a neatly pressed white shirt, and a bow tie, swept up the cash with a push broom.

LaShune rose to her feet and damn near fell. I figured she must've been bent off the liquor 'cause she had been drinking since morning. She tossed dollar bills at the chick and started to sing along and dance to the chorus. "I ain't gotta nigga, I'm throwed on that liquor, I'm 'bout to hit the club, And dance like a stripper..." She stepped up closer to the girl and yelled, "Bend over, baby, so I can tip you." Red Bottom bent over and shook her ass. LaShune swiped her credit card down the chick's ass and said, "Bitch, I ain't got no more cash." Zoned off the alcohol, LaShune thought it was funny, but the stripper climbed down from the stage, got in LaShune's grill, balled her fist, and connected it to her nose. LaShune's mouth flew open. "Trick, I'm 'bout to go silly on yo' ass." Before she could strike, Rich bounced to his feet and pushed Red Bottom away from LaShune so hard that she fell to the floor.

Four huge bouncers stormed over, grabbed Rich and LaShune, and escorted them away. Red Bottom finally rose up. That's when I tapped Jia on the leg and said, "I'm out." I grabbed her hand and started toward the door.

Confused, Jia asked, "What's up with your friend's girl?"

I ignored her question and kept walking. I was too heated to say anything back. We walked through the crowd until we got outside in the lot. LaShune and Rich were standing by the car alone, going back and forth.

"You kno' better than sliding that card up that bitch's ass. Everywhere you go you got to drink then you ready to show yo' ass," Rich fussed, all up in her face.

She waved him off. "Nigga, get out my face. You ain't my damn daddy, and I don't need you poppin' off at the mouth 'bout how I act. If you wanna train something, go get you a puppy and teach that mothafucka how to act. I'm not wit' this bullshit you goin' on and on about," she snapped back.

I unlocked the whip. Rich let his front seat up and snatched LaShune up by the arm. "Hoe, get in the goddamn car," he ordered before forcing her in. She tried to object and tried to release his grip but was no match for him.

She kicked at his leg. "I ain't no child, and I damn sho' ain't yours," she spazzed. Everybody else got in, and I pulled off. On the highway, the arguing didn't get any better.

"You better start praying 'cause when we get back to the condo you gon' get right," Rich warned from the passenger seat.

"Tsk, you ain't gon' do nothing but run yo' mouth 'cause you ain't gon' run me." LaShune didn't back down. Rich finally killed their argument by being silent. The ride home was a quiet one after that; I didn't even turn the radio on. I just needed to think and cool off. Rich needed to teach LaShune how to act in public. There was no coming up with a bitch like that in his corner. Her mouth would make a nigga put a fist to her dome. Had it been one of my bitches that got out of pocket, she'd be on her way to get her head stitched up.

Meeting With The Devil

Stephanie

Ashley held a blank expression on her face, and I heard the echo of the bullet as it struck Marcus' head. He let out a hysterical cry, a blanket of red blood splattered all over me right before his body fell to the floor. I closed my eyes to keep out the gory image that had played in front of me. I re-opened my eyes when I heard her say, "I told this nigga to stop playin' with me. Guess he didn't think I would kill his ass." She stood over him staring with no remorse.

Blood gushed from the hole in his temple like a waterfall and stained the beige carpet. He had been once alive and suddenly he was laying there dead. Ashley aimed the gun at me and pulled the trigger again. At first, I didn't feel anything, and I wondered if I had really been shot. I no longer had to wonder when I looked to the side and saw blood oozing from my shoulder. My shoulder began to get hot, and the pain shot through it, feeling like I was being stabbed with a knife. I planted my hand over my wound and laid down hoping that I would be able to make it out of there.

Ashley's eyes and mine locked, and then she pointed the nine milli at her head. Pow! She dropped to the floor on her back and laid there stiff as a board. The gun landed by her feet. I had a feeling that she would never get back up again. She had killed her husband, shot me, and committed suicide. I had watched two people be shot right in front of me. I had to get some help and fast.

I reached over to the phone on the nightstand in excruciating pain and dialed the emergency number, trembling and in shock.

As soon as the female operator answered, I began to speak. "I've been shot, and I think the two people in here are dead," I slowly slurred into the receiver."

"Ma'am, I have an ambulance on the way," she quickly said. After that, everything went blank.

Tempers Flare

Sayveon

I told Jia goodbye once I got back to the condo. I gave her a hug and said, "My bad 'bout what happened tonight. I wanted you to enjoy yo' self wit' out the bullshit interfering. I'm really diggin' yo' style and if it's good wit' you, I want to take you out to dinner tomorrow." I rubbed her arm, and she didn't stop me from copping a feel.

"I'm down with that and don't worry about what happened tonight. It's okay, and I won't hold that against you," she said back. I moved my hand up and gently played with her hair. I stared into her pretty browns and then kissed her cheek and moved down to her neck. I slowly moved my left hand to her lower back and then to her soft ass. I slightly tilted my head to the right and tongued her down.

I ended the kiss by slowly pulling back. She smiled before she made a few steps over to her snow-white four- door Audi A-7 sedan, slid in, and drove a few buildings over back to her condo.

I took a deep breath and went into the condo where Rich and LaShune were. As soon as I opened the door, I had to hear the bullshit. They both stood in the living room staring each other down and tossing insults back and forth.

"Bitch, I made you. You didn't have shit when I got wit' you. Now you wanna show yo' ass and get brand new on me talking out the side of yo' neck and talking slick out the mouth. You better stay in yo' place, or I'm gon' put you in it," Rich growled.

"I was a self-made bitch when I met yo' stupid ass. And, I say what the fuck I want to. God blessed me wit' a mouth, and I'm gon' use this mothafucka. I don't kno' what kind of lame ass bitches you was fucking wit' before me, but *this* is not *that* sweetie. Boss up and do something," she provoked. She upped the freshly done nail of her pointer finger and pressed it into his forehead.

"Y'all chill on all that befo' a neighbor calls the popo's. We don't need them kind of problems up in here," I intervened, tryna calm shit down.

What I said had no effect on Rich because he wailed on LaShune with a mean right hook knocking her down to the floor. It was about time 'cause he had been handling her with kid gloves in the car. LaShune laid on the floor, holding her cheek. Rich stood over her talking through clenched teeth. "Bitch, you gon' learn to stop poppin' yo' gums." He snatched her up, grabbed her by the throat, and pinned her against the wall. Her feet were dangling in mid air. LaShune kneed him in the groin; he didn't flinch. All of a sudden, he hurled her across the room, and she smashed into the wall. She lay in the corner, gasping air.

Finally, she stood up and swung off on Rich. "Don't you ever do that shit again," she fumed. She ran into the back and came out with a hammer. They were wildin', and I tried not to get in the mix of their shit.

I stood to the side, if Rich didn't check his bitch soon, I knew I would have to step in and stop the fuck shit they had goin' on.

LaShune went on a rampage. She smashed the fridge with the hammer and then attempted to hit the wall before Rich pinned her arms down and snatched the tool from her hand. Rich left out of the condo and yelled over his shoulder, "I'm done fucking wit' you after tonight, hoe." He slammed the door.

I walked into the room and layed down across the bed. I heard the door slam to Rich's room. LaShune had gotten the ass whoopin' that was long overdue. I chilled out, thinking 'bout Jia and how I would tear her pussy walls down the first opportunity I got.

After The Black Out

Stephanie

I woke up to a bright light in my face, and I heard voices around me. I slowly opened my eyes and blinked. That's when I realized I was on a gurny being rolled into an ambulance.

"Ma'am can you give me your name?" the female paramedic asked, staring down at me with her dark green eyes and brunette hair.

"Ste---pha---nie Da---vis," I slowly murmured.

"Okay, Ms. Davis. We're taking you to the hospital to get some help. Just stay calm. We're headed there now," she said. Outside, I could feel sprinkles of raindrops falling down on me. The sound of the thunder and lightning rang in my ears and made me slightly jump. The female paramedic smiled and assured, "It's alright."

That was the longest ambulance drive I ever wanted to have. We were in a thunderstorm, and the driver was having difficulty trying to keep the vehicle from sliding on the highway. I felt a few jerks, and I could hear the water splashing under the tires when he hit a water puddle. I couldn't do anything but lay there and think. As I contemplated my situation, my thoughts drifted to my boys. I might never see them again, not even to say goodbye. The adrenaline from that had me nervous and scared. I gently closed my eyes and went to a whole 'nother place.

An angel accompanied me and took me outside of the gate of heaven. There were two other beautiful angels standing there. They were clothed in glistening robes, and their faces gleamed with light. The angel that brought me over ordered, "Stay right here, Stephanie, and I'll be right back." He left me standing while he went over and spoke to the angels guarding the entrance. The gate slowly opened. My guiding angel escorted me through the magnificent gate and into heaven. Suddenly, soft beautiful music filled the air all around me. A powerful wave of stunning sound surged the air and seemed to envelope everything and everyone.

The angel that guided me softly gripped my hand and led me to the city. The sight of it was breath taking. The landscaping was indescribable. The flowers were the most colorful I'd ever seen. There was unbelievable greenery and vegetation everywhere.

Citizens of heaven happily wandered around looking like they had peace and joy. They also wore pure white robes. Families and friends joined together laughing and talking among each other. Everyone was doing something, going somewhere, or conversing and smiling. A glow covered every face that I saw. I was happy to see my grandparents, my mother's parents, who came over and hugged me. Big Ma looked angelic, and Big Papa smiled and gave me a kiss on the cheek. "You're still my li'l sunshine," he told me. That was my nickname from him. They both left the earth only six months apart when I was fourteen. Seeing the two of them put a wide smile on my face. My granddad looked over his shoulder. "Your momma is around here somewhere with your daddy."

Next thing I knew, I began to shed tears of joy. My parents appeared before me holding hands. My mother held a baby in her arms. I ran up to them and held them tight. "Oh God, I missed y'all so much." I looked at the handsome li'l boy in her arms and asked, "Who's this?"

"We're glad to see you too. This is your li'l brother, Seth. He died at six months before you were born." Seth looked just like me and Sparkle. He surely was my bro. She laughed from excitement, but her smile quickly left. I wondered what was wrong. "It's not your time yet, baby. You need to go back," she ordered and gave me a slight push in the other direction.

"Noooooo! Mama, I want to be with you and daddy," I whined and grabbed a hold of her robe. She used her hand to pry my hands away from hers. After that, I saw nothing but white. Everything was a blur.

Certified Freak Status

Sayveon

I had just dozed off when the door cracked open and a glow of dim light from the kitchen entered the room. I thought I was dreaming til' I noticed a body standing there holding something in its hand. The body stepped over and turned on the lamp beside the bed where I was. She made a circle, showing off her purple see-through teddy. Underneath the supa short lingerie was a pair of matching purple thongs. "You like my fit?" she asked, smiling like she was cheesing for a picture.

Irritated from the light and wondering where the hell Rich was I said, "Ay, what the fuck you got goin' on? Where yo' nigga at?" I looked her up and down, this hoe was a freak fa real.

"He ain't come back yet. I decided to come and keep you company while he's gon'. Don't worry 'bout that bastard. I already locked the front door so his ass can't get in." She sat a small bucket on the dresser and stepped to me. She turned the light off, leaned over on me, and licked down my neck. She reached over in the container and put something in her mouth. I knew it was ice when I felt a cool wetness make circles all over my chest. She wrapped her cold tongue around my navel. I readjusted the pillow under my head and let her make her way down to the head of my stick. I didn't object. I let her get it in. She purred like a kitten while she sucked up and down my dick.

"Nakia or that Chinese bitch you met can't do it like this, huh?" she managed to ask, slurping up and down the shaft of my dick. The warmth of her tongue combined with the coolness of the ice cube was making me feel like busting off down her throat. I gripped a handful of her hair and pushed her head down further on my piece. Instead of gagging, she deep throated every inch of my shit. She locked her jaws and pulled even harder on my rod til I shot off.

"Mmm---dang yo' cum taste like cherries," she said, swallowed my babies, wiped her mouth with the palm of her hand and turned to go. "Before I go I want to put a bug in your ear. Nakia's baby ain't yours. It's her husband's, and he's back living there with her. I'm putting you up on the skinny 'cause you need to kno' what's up and not come there and there be some problems," she released and walked out.

I thought about what she had just told me and wondered if LaShune was being real when she said the baby may not be mine. I could believe it 'cause I caught dude over there at her house. I knew LaShune couldn't really be trusted though. She had been giving me head service and 'twat' since I had been in Miami, and I hadn't forgotten how she sucked my dick back in 'The Sipp' when Nakia went to the store. Until I knew fo' sho' that Nakia's baby was mine, I had made up my mind that she wouldn't get no more talk from me.

I went into the bathroom and wiped my dick off before going back to bed. I fell off to sleep when I heard about three knocks at the front. I knew it was

Rich trying to get back in. I grumbled low, "Damn. Nigga knockin' like he the police."

I heard LaShune open her room door, and I could hear her footsteps going to the front to let Rich in. I heard an unfamiliar voice inside the living room, and then LaShune let out a loud scream. I jumped up, grabbed my steel, and ran into the living room. The two mothafuckas I laid eyes on had me trippin' and wondering what the fuck they wanted.

The Truth Is Out There

Sayveon

I placed my heater out of eyesight in a spot by the living room door and asked, "What's goin' on?"

LaShune was shook up and didn't say nothing. The older of the white cops turned around to face me. "Are you her boyfriend's friend?" he nodded his head over toward LaShune's way, referring to her.

"Yeah," I made known.

"I asked if she had someone here to comfort her, and she told me that her boyfriend's friend was in there asleep." He made a few steps over to where I stood. "Well, I'm sorry, but I brought some bad news here this morning. Her boyfriend, Sirlentay Adkins, was found murdered outside of The Hilton downtown on Biscayne Boulevard along with a female by the name of Jacqueline Sanchez," he notified.

I walked in the room and sat on the sofa. I peered over on the table in the ashtray to see whether the blunt Rich smoked earlier had been moved. Somebody had snatched it up, and it was all to the good 'cause we didn't need the po's starting shit. My mind went back to what I had heard. This shit was crazy. I needed to get the low-down on what happened.

"What went on wit' 'em?" I needed to kno'.

The older officer with Officer Neal Griffin on his nametag did all the talking. "Well, Sirlentay and Jacqueline were gunned down leaving a hotel room early this morning. Another guest at the room called us and reported that they heard gunshots and screams in the parking lot, and two people were down. When we got there, they both didn't have a pulse and had been shot in the head. Jacqueline's car was registered to this address and was in Al Rodriguez's name. What kinship do the two of them have?" he asked.

"Al, is her kids' daddy," I said and then froze on giving out any more info.

"We are going to need the next of kin to come down and identify the bodies. If possible, can you all call the families and have them to call me as soon as possible?" he asked and handed me a card with his name and phone number on it.

"Aight," I said.

The cop turned to LaShune. "I'm sorry this happened."

Both police left out of the condominium.

LaShune boo hooed and was on her way to the back room when she dropped to her knees. "I can't believe he's gone. Then, he was fucking another bitch while he was down here."

I walked pass her and went into the bedroom to get my cell. Fuck that bitch and her crying over her nigga fucking Jackie. I was worried about how Pops would take the news. Then, it hit me. When Pops was telling me and Rich that he wanted us to check up on Jackie, Rich made a bogus remark. It was all adding up. He had prob'ly been fucking Jackie the whole time, and the baby might've been his.

I grabbed my phone from the bed and walked outside to dial Pops. The phone rang at least six times before he answered in a groggy tone. "Hello," he spoke.

"Pops, Jackie and Rich been killed. The popo left here about five minutes ago and said they got shot in the heads this morning," I let out.

"Where were they killed?" he asked.

I hesitated first, and then said, "Outside a hotel." I didn't want to put my boy on the spot, but it it is what it is.

Pops didn't speak for a few seconds before asking, "Did you take care of my people since you've been down there?" He was speaking of the move me and Rich made with the Cubans when we dropped off the kilos.

"Very good. Aren't you coming back soon?"

"Yeah, I'm gon' leave out later today. I'll see you when I get back, and I'm gon' cop me a new ride when I get back too," I let him know.

"Good deal, son. I'll see you soon."

We both hung up. The fucked up part of the whole conversation with Pops was that he wasn't stressing over his ole' lady being dead. I had a feeling that Pops had that set up, damn. Now I had to watch my back more than I already had been. Shit, he could have had a hit out on me too for fucking his daughter. I chilled out and stopped with the paranoia. It was all good I wasn't worried.

Putting Up A Strong Fight

Stephanie

Everything moved in slow motion when Ashley appeared in my hospital room aiming the nine milli at my temple. She stared directly into my eyes. "I'm killing you this time, bitch," she threatened. Her baseball cap, shirt, pants, and shoes were all black and the look on her face told me that she meant business this time.

"You're supposed to be dead. Why are you doing this?" I asked, shivering under the thin white sheet on the bed.

"I ain't dead, but you 'bout to be." She pulled the trigger of the gun. Pop! Pop! Pop! The noise from the sound of the weapon when it went off made the whole room shake, quacking the floor.

I screamed to the top of my voice. "Nurse! Nurse! Nurse! Help me, please!"

I woke up from the nightmare and heard voices but couldn't understand what they were saying. There were blurred images of faces peering down at me and then they moved away. Darkness came, and my consciousness faded in and out. One minute I was at Marcus' house for dinner and the next my body was being moved around and placed in an ambulance. I laid there groaning from the pain in my shoulder and trying to replay in my head what all had happened.

Gradually, things became clearer, and I became a bit more aware of my surroundings and my condition. In my arm, I could see an IV. Sparkle and a nurse came over to me. I tried to speak to my sister. "H...i..." I pronounced as slow as a snail's pace. When I did that, I created lots of commotion.

"She's awake," Sparkle said smiling and waving at me.

"Let me go and get the doctor," the nurse said.

The tall Caucasian doctor came in right away. "Do you know your name?" he asked.

I nodded. "Stephanie--- Davis," I was able to say.

Everyone but Sparkle left out of the room. I wondered, Is Marcus living? Am I going to be okay? When would I be able to go home?

A stocky and short CNA came into the room. "I need to change her," she told Sparkle who moved aside.

I almost lost it. I lay there thinking, What the fuck is she talkin' bout? I know damn well this woman ain't saying that I'm up here shitting and pissing on myself. I frowned. When she came close, I started to fidget, and I swung off on her. That made my shoulder hurt like hell, but there was no way that I wanted this chick cleaning my 'cooch' and wiping my ass. Oh hell nawl. "Damn, am I this bad off?" I thought to myself.

The CNA looked at Sparkle. "I don't think she will let me clean her up."

"I'll help you. She's just afraid because she doesn't know you," Sparkle said. I saw her put on a pair a gloves from the glove container on the wall. Then, she helped the Cna slowly turn me on my side and give me my bed bath while she comforted me the whole time saying, "It's okay, sis, we're only trying to get you cleaned up." I did feel slightly better knowing that my sis was in the room with me, being supportive and making sure I was good. I never would have dreamed that I would be in the hospital getting a birdbath after almost being killed by a psychopath.

Damn, life had a funny way of sneaking up on you with the unexpected and making you appreciate what you lost. I had lost my independence, but I wouldn't stop until I got it back. If I could beat a drug addiction, this would be simple, a small thing to a giant.

About an hour had passed after my bed bath. Even though it hurt me to move around and get cleaned up, I felt fresher. I slowly turned toward the window smelling like fresh baby powder and lotion. The beautiful sunlight shined in the room, and the baby blue sky added to the beauty. I tried to enjoy the scenery, but the strong pain medicine that I had recently had injected in the IV had me sleepy as hell. The doctor left the bullet in my shoulder. He explained to me that the bullet may be pressed against a damaged blood vessel and removing it might have caused severe bleeding. I had gone through a lot of stupidity in the last twelve hours and I finally had gotten a break.

I heard a familiar voice speak to Sparkle. "Hey, mama. You good?" the voice asked. I slowly twisted my neck toward the door and tears of joy shed when I noticed my two boys standing in the room. Jacob came over and kissed me on my forehead.

I smiled. "Hey, baby," I said. My voice had finally gotten strong enough for me to talk.

My other son, Jacob, gave me a kiss on the cheek. "You look beautiful, mama," he said, even though I knew he was only being sweet. There was no way I looked nice laying up in a hospital bed after being shot.

Jacob sat at the foot of the bed and suddenly broke down. The terrible hurt that came over me is indescribable. I couldn't do anything to comfort him at a time when he really needed me. "I already lost my daddy. My mama's in the hospital from being shot, and I feel like giving up. I must be being punished for some shit I don't kno' about. I'm in school trying to do everything right," he sobbed. He held his head down and let it all out in the palms of his hands.

Sparkle soothed her nephew by rubbing up and down his back. "It's okay, Jacob. You are gonna be okay. Don't worry about it."

His brother's eyes teared up, and he stepped out into the hallway. Jason rarely showed emotion.

He had never been good at expressing himself. He reminded me so much of James with not only his looks but his attitude as well. My baby son reminded me more of me with his behavior and the way he let out however he felt. He always humbled himself more. Although they had different attitudes and were like night and day, I loved them the same.

"I love you, Mama and Aunt Sparkle. I'll do anything for y'all," he said in tears.

"I love you, too," I said in a low tone, hurting inside because I had already done enough damage to my kids by not being there for them when I was incarcerated. Now was the time for me to do better and be the mother that they wanted and needed. It seemed that I had let them down.

"C'mere," I told Jason. He scooted up to where I laid. I put his head on my stomach and I rubbed his head. "You're just a big ole' baby," I joked.

He slightly smiled and wiped his eyes with the sheet. I hadn't been the best mother, but I promised myself that morning that I would make good choices because what I did not only affected me, but also my family.

Days Later

Stephanie

The guilt consuming my insides overwhelmed me with shame. I kept blaming myself for the death of my boy's daddy. I continued to say to myself that I should have found him some help after I learned that he started back using smack.

James' mother and sister hated me, thinking I had something to do with his death. Neither one told me about the funeral. Grandma Annie invited me, but I felt so unwelcomed as I walked discreetly into the dim lighting. My eyes were brimmed with tears causing my vision to be blurred. James occasionally attended that Catholic Church. He had gone there every since he was a youngster with his grandmother.

There was a vast amount of people there and the sobs, sniffles, cries, and moans made up most of the murmuring drone that swept around the cathedral. I began to walk slowly down the center aisle of the church following James' immediate family. My kids and Sparkle walked down with me. I endured every step with the upmost pain running through my veins. The interior of the building made it beautiful. The atmosphere in it was a mixture of tragic rage and pure sadness, blended together to make an invisible heavy shadow over me. My slow movements were like a drunk woman. I hadn't shut my eyes the night before. I could hardly steady my steps and felt grief from head to toe. That was a sad day. It seemed like the life had been sucked out of me.

There it was in front of me, right in front of the altar, top open. An all black casket trimmed in gold enclosed around the body of what was and would never be again: a loving man. I made my way cautiously toward the body. James had on a slim fit gray suit looking peaceful with his eyes closed. I stared at his lips because I knew they would never move again and I'd never be able to listen to his voice again which only made the image more surreal. There was nothing real left of him, no life or energy. He had been transformed into a useless lump of chilly flesh, waiting for its time to rot away. The thought of that tore my heart out. It had hurt the boys too because they stood over their father staring at his face with streams of tears falling. We had our crying moment before I decided that it was time for me to move away from the corpse.

As I moved a foot to go on to be seated, I felt a hand on my sore shoulder that caused a trickle of pain to shoot through it. I shifted my head slightly to see his grandmother, Annie, draining every drop of water in her body through her eyes, nearly bloodshot. Her mouth came within an inch of my ear, and she whispered, "I'm glad you could make it."

I smiled. "Thanks for being sweet enough to tell me about the funeral."

"You know you're my girl, and I love you," she sweetly said wearing a black dress suit and a black wide brimmed hat. She looked nice for her age and if I didn't know her I'd never have guessed that she's in her early eighties.

She went on and sat on the front pew with James' mother who looked me from head to toe, frowned, rolled her eyes, and looked off. Atasha sat right next to the mother, and she rolled her eyes as well. *Stank bitches!* I was not in the mood for the foolishness. I didn't entertain it. Glenda smiled the second she spotted Jacob and Jason. They went over and hugged her neck and ended up sitting on the front row with her. The funeral home director directed everyone to the pews, and I was finally seated on the third row side by side with Sparkle.

The tall African American priest who wore a charcoal-black robe waited for the casket to be closed before he sprinkled holy water on top, and another person placed a white pall over it. I could barely remember anything that happened during the funeral. It was like I was dreaming. I only remembered the concluding prayer. The priest stood there and said, "God, our shelter and strength, you listen in love to the cry of your people. Hear the prayers we offer for our departed brother, James, and grant him the fullness of redemption. We ask this through Christ our Lord."

The congregation spoke, Amen.

Everyone was told to stand, and the body was wheeled down the aisle, put in the hearse, and taken to Saint Mary Of The Springs Catholic Cemetery in Camden, Mississippi. Most of their family was buried there, and James always told me that he wanted to be placed there too. Sparkle drove me there with Jacob and Jason riding on the backseat. She trailed behind the funeral home car until we made it to the burial grounds that could be found on a dirt road. A silver gate surrounded the huge graveyard. I got out of the SUV thinking of all the people who once had a body and soul and now they were bones and dust. I wondered how many had been forgotten by family and friends who only mourned for a short while and eventually moved on with their lives. I promised myself that no matter what went on in my future, I would at least keep flowers on James' grave. I planned to visit whenever I could.

The immediate family sat right in front of the grave while a big crowd stood in the back. The priest said a prayer, and it wasn't long before the body was lowered in the ground. He said, "We therefore commit, James to the ground. Earth to earth, ashes to ashes, dust to dust, in the sure and certain hope of the Resurrection to eternal life." And, it was over.

The people huddled in small groups afterwards, talking to one another. I stood by the gate and off to myself. I was still in shock and couldn't believe that all of that was happening. He would never come back home.

James' auntie, Linda, came over. "Hi, baby. I hope it gets better for you and the boys." She rubbed my arm.

"Thank you. I hope it does too," I said to her. Linda hugged my sons and went on about her business.

I slowly turned to Sparkle. "I'm ready to go before my shoulder starts hurting. I didn't bring my pain meds."

"Okay, let's roll."

I was about to head to the gate's entrance when I heard, "You got a lot of nerve to show up here knowing I don't like yo' ass." I knew it was Glenda, James' mother.

I waved her off. "I'm not goin' there with you today, Glenda."

The next thing I knew, Atasha was standing beside her and put her two cents in. "This hoe musta forgot that we'll whoop her ass."

Sparkle cut in. "I'm not going to let anybody touch my sister, and y'all ain't shit. James prob'ly turning over in his grave knowing instead of y'all hoes mourning, y'all starting shit and tryna fight."

"Mind ya business, bitch," Atasha snapped at Sparkle and slid out of her slip-in shoes and stood there in a silver two piece pants suit, ready for whatever.

Sparkle didn't fold, she shot back, "My sister is my business. I'ma let you kno this, if you buck, I'm fucking you up."

"Don't threaten me," Atasha growled and pushed Sparkle.

"Spark, just leave it alone. These bitches ain't worth it. Let it go," I tried to persuade and tugged her arm.

Sparkle wasn't tryna hear that, she snatched away and swung off on Atasha who couldn't get a throw in. "I'm 'bout to Molly Whop you, bitch!" Sparkle yelled while she put the beat down on her. Atasha took a blow to the head, slipped down on another grave, and hit her skull on the tombstone, which dazed her and then knocked her out cold. Jacob grabbed Sparkle and held her until she calmed down.

"Let her go. It's my turn, and I'm 'bout to put a good old fashioned country ass whoopin' on you, hoe," Glenda bragged, talking to Sparkle and jumping her humongous ass all around like she was an Olympic boxer in the ring.

While Jacob held on to Sparkle, Jason grabbed his grandmother who swung and kicked like a lunatic trying to get away to attack my sister. Jason pushed and blocked her to keep her from his auntie. He had wrestled with her so much that she ended up close to his dad's grave where two workers had shovels placing the dirt on top. The last push was too hard and one of her legs ended up falling down in her son's grave that was half-full of dirt. "Oooow!" Glenda hollered. Several people including the priest helped her out of the hole. At first, I didn't think it was funny until Sparkle went down to one knee laughing. I burst out cracking up and heard snickering coming from the mouths of other lookers.

Glenda stood there angry and upset. "Y'all mothafuckas done tried me today," she said. Her sister, Linda, handed her a Kleenex. Glenda snatched it and wiped the dirt off her face. She took off the drawstring ponytail she had on. The short real hair on her head was sticking straight up and she looked like a troll. With no shame, she shook it from side to side, shaking all of the dusty dirt from it and clamped her ponytail back on.

The priest walked over. "I need all of you to leave the premises. Not only is this disrespectful to the deceased, but its disrespectful to God. You should all be ashamed and I'll be sure to send up a prayer for each of you. You're going to surely need it," he said in a disgusted tone and walked away.

Me and my family got together and hauled ass. It was sad that me and Glenda couldn't and hadn't ever gotten along. I hated the way things happened that day which was supposed to be the day we celebrated a life, instead we created a disaster. Then again, I think a lesson was learned for Atasha. She should've learned that if she issued a lick, she better be able to take one. Well, in her case take a bunch of 'em.

A Saturday Afternoon Shocker

Sparkle

After James' funeral, all I wanted to do was come home and relax. It had been a long morning for me, and I couldn't take any more of the extra shit. Mothafuckas were forever trying to test me, and I'd had enough of it. I was mad at the world until I walked through the door. Aunt Ruby stood there holding Layla in her arms. Layla's smile made me forget about how angry I was, but the upset look on Auntie's face notified me that something was wrong.

I took Layla from Aunt Ruby and asked, "What's wrong?"

She placed her hand on her hip. "I've been looking for Harry and I can't find him. I haven't seen him in days."

I looked away and then back at her. The guilt was eating me up, but there was no way I would tell her that her rooster was dead. "I don't know where he is. I hope a coyote hasn't gotten a hold of him," I lied, knowing good and well that his mean ass was in Rooster Hell prob'ly running around pecking anything in his way.

"This has really hurt me. I guess an old dog or something might have come along and eaten him up." She held her head down for a minute and walked away. "I'm 'bout to wash dishes and make a blackberry pie," she said and went into the kitchen.

I thought to myself that I should buy her a gift to cheer her up. I would do something nice for her later.

I heard a few knocks at the door and asked, "Who is it?"

"Ontavious," the deep voice answered, my stomach quivered from nervousness. The last time I laid eyes on him, he basically put me out of his house and called me a liar.

I opened the door,, and we greeted one another. He reached for Layla and she dove into his arms, all smiles. We both had a seat on the sofa, and it was quiet for a while, almost like we didn't know what to say to each other.

"Did you go ahead with the abortion?" he asked, breaking the silence between us.

"Yes."

He nodded. "I guess you did what was best." He put Layla down on the floor with a few of the colored blocks she played with. He looked directly into my eyes. "Baby, I know you probably were afraid to tell me about the pregnancy, but I'm not that type of dude that you have to hide information from. I will love you regardless of what happened in your past. If we keep the lines of communication open, we can face almost any problem. The truth will never hurt me. It's the lies that can kill what we're trying to build."

I looked away then down to the floor. He used his hand to hold my head up, and we looked deep into each other's eyes. "I'm sorry," I whispered, my voice had gotten weak from my emotions. I missed him so much and was saddened that my one mistake led to our misunderstanding. "I didn't know how to tell you, but I will be totally honest from now on. I'm not trying to lose you. You mean the world to me and I love the fact that not only do you love me, you love my daughter. I love you, baby."

He smiled. "I love you, too."

He embraced me. "So, you're not mad at me anymore?" I asked.

"No." He kissed me on the lips and held my hand. I heard voices coming from outside and realized that they were singing. I hopped up from the sofa and opened the door.

Three tall and handsome men began to sing. "All my life... I prayed for someone like you... and I thank God that I finally found you..." My heartbeat sped up, and I wondered what the heck was going on with the tall and handsome men singing at my doorstep.

Ontavious opened the door and let the dudes in. They continued to sing the entire song by K-Ci and Jo-Jo, 'All My Life.' Then he grabbed my hand, went into his pocket, and pulled out a small blue velvet box. "These last few days made me realize that I don't want to live without you. I promise to love you and remain faithful. I feel that you're the one for me and no other woman compares to you. I promise to protect you and never hurt you intentionally or betray your trust. You complete me and make me happy. By accepting this ring, you promise to do the same. Do you accept the ring?" He opened the box and pulled out a heart shaped pink- diamond promise ring.

Tears poured down, and I hugged his neck tightly. "Yes, baby."

He whispered in my ear. "From here on out, lets grow together. You been on my mind so much. I don't know what you've done to me, but you got me going crazy."

Laughing I whispered back, "It's the coochie, sweetie." We both burst out laughing. He picked me up hugging me. My legs wrapped around his waist, and we passionately kissed.

"We came to sing the song not watch all of this," one of the men teased.

"These are my cousins, baby. They have a singing group, and I asked them to sing for us today," he introduced. They all said hello, and Ontavious thanked them.

Right before they left, Aunt Ruby came in with her pink apron wrapped around her waist. She looked at Ontavius. "I see you did what you said you were gon' do." She smiled, showing off her gold grill.

I put my hand on my hip. "Auntie, you knew about this?"

"I sho' did."

Auntie looked at my ring. "Oh, that's pretty. Next you can ask her to marry you."

We both looked at her and smiled because Auntie was something else with herself. Ontavious introduced her to his cousins, and they left. I had a rough day, but something good happened later on. After all that I had gone through in my past relationship, I never thought that I would find a good man who would love me and treat me with respect. I guess that saying is true, 'It gets greater, later.'

Final Respects Back In The Sipp

Sayveon

At one o'clock that Saturday evening, I attended the funeral of my boy, Rich. We walked into the church, and his mother made sure I got blessed with a seat on the second row. The pews were packed with people who cared for him, knew him, and wanted to pay their respects. Hundreds of mourners gathered that day, and a huge crowd that couldn't fit inside stood outside.

As I sat directly behind the immediate family, I was able to discreetly observe. I watched his mother's shoulders heave and shake. Rich's dad placed his arm around her and comforted her. The pain of seeing her hurting made it hard to look at her grieving. She had only one son and daughter. Her only son lay in front of her in a dark black and silver casket. Her daughter, Bridget, kept fidgeting and was constantly glancing around. Her gaze swept across the filled up church. She quickly focused on the choir when they stood and sang a hymn called, 'Precious Lord,' the same tune sang at most black funerals.

The soloist stood off to the side with the microphone and began humming a tune before singing the song. She had an angelic voice that sounded sweet and pure. I wasn't the kind to be moved by church music, but ole' girl had my full attention. She could sing circles around some of the well-known recording artists in the industry. When she finished her song, the minister stood and preached the eulogy. At the end, he asked anyone who would like to say something about the deceased to come forward.

Bridget walked up to the stand. She was highly educated and had a Master's Degree in Early Childhood Development. She began to read from a piece of paper in her hand while holding the mic. "My brother, Sirlentay, lived each day to the fullest, and he inspired me to do the same. His adventurous attitude, his broad range of interest, and his happy demeanor made him a wonderful man to know. He was generous with his time and affection. He always took an interest in the people he met. There were few people that he couldn't engage in conversation at any time or place. I introduced him to several of my friends over the years, and they always told me how cool he'd been. My brother pursued his many endeavors diligently and always rose to meet a challenge. I always felt that he expected the same from me. Not having my big brother will be a great challenge, but I know he lives in my heart."

She turned to the casket and a tear fell from her watery eyes. "I'll miss his perspective on life and his gentle humor. I'll miss the surprising depth and scope of his knowledge. I'll miss the warmth he extended. I will miss my brother dearly, but I will treasure his memory right here forever," she said, pointing at her heart. The mother sniffled and broke down into tears from Bridget's final words. Bridget went back to where she sat and the preacher asked if anyone else would like to come up.

LaShune stood and wobbled her drunk ass up to say some words wearing a brown mini-dress, fishnet stockings, and high-heeled pumps looking like the definition of ratchet. She pulled the shades up that covered her eyes. "Y'all have to excuse me. I'm so upset right now." She smacked her lips and sighed. "Me and Rich were just chilling in Miami when this went down. I can't believe he's gone." She wiped tears from her eyes. "My condokency..." She cleared her throat and paused for a minute. "I hope I said that word right. Anyway, they go out to his mama, daddy, and sister. I pray that thangs get better for y'all, soon." She glanced over at the casket. "Rest in peace, boo." She pulled her shades back down before staggering back to her seat beside her sister, Nakia.

LaShune tried to be proper, but didn't even know how to pronounce condolences. Dayum, shorty-girl stayed hitting the bottle. It was a damn shame. Bridget and her mother shook their heads. I know they had to be glad when she sat down.

The person who went up next from the front pew didn't look familiar. I had never seen her before. I figured it must have been a cousin or something like that. The woman started to speak, "At the end of the day, every man wonders if he has made his wife and kids proud. My husband made me proud, and our young son and daughter are proud of him as well. I met Sirlentay right after I graduated from college. We had the same hopes and dreams and got married and had two beautiful children and one on the way." Her swollen belly showed that she had to be about eight months from the way she wobbled when she walked.

She wiped away a tear with a finger and continued. "We separated three years ago, but a year ago we fell in love all over again. He's gone, but he's blessed me with three special gifts that I will always love and cherish. Both his family and many friends will sorely miss him. As he rests from his life's labor, this great husband, father, son, brother, and friend should know that he made his family proud." She and her kids who looked to be about six and eight, and were the spitting image of their daddy, sat right back beside the in- laws.

Out of the corner of my eye, I could see LaShune sitting across the aisle from me looking stupid with her mouth hanging open. She let out, "What the..." Nakia quickly used her hand to cover her sister's mouth. People looked over at the interruption that they had going on, but some music started to play that blocked out the commotion that could have erupted and 'caused some problems.

The male from the choir took the microphone and sang, 'Go Rest High On That Mountain.' My eyes were probably the only dry eyes in the house after that song. Even I felt the sadness from the words. Afterwards, the pianist played a tune, and the preacher said, "At this time we will allow family members, family, and friends to view the body."

Rich's mother stood there by the corpse sobbing and hollering, "My---b---a---b---y..." Her husband pulled her away and out of church. She left out screaming and boo-hooing. When it was time for me to view, I went up and looked down. Rich was swagged up in a black tuxedo with a red vest. He looked like he had just taken a nap and would get up later and hit the streets, hustlin'. That's what he did best. I knew that would be the last time I saw him, and I went out. Outside, men and women wore 'RIP Rich' t-shirts with his picture. On the pic my boy stood by his new-modeled black Navigator on chrome shoes. Others flashed gang signs and exchanged gang handshakes because Rich was affiliated wit' the 'Four Corner Hustlers'. The four is pronounced, 'fo.' 4CH's are a faction of 'The Vice Lords.' He had his people standing behind him fo' sho', reppin' to the fullest.

The majority of outsiders danced and sang along to Master P's lyrics, 'Miss My Homies,' that was hitting hard from a sound system. The crowd sang, "Sitting at the ghetto thinking 'bout, All my homies passed away, Candy painted Cadillac's and triple gold, That's how me and my boys roll..." The parking lot dance party was a testament of how much he was loved in Jackson, Mississippi. It showed how much he was respected, known, and appreciated. While the mourners sang, pallbearers loaded the casket into the black hearse.

The funeral procession meandered to Mount Calvary cemetery a mile away. A white car in front of us fired shots. Other niggas waved guns out of the windows, held up liquor bottles, and swerved in and out of traffic, wildin'. Fucked up as it sounds, this was how soldiers showed their love when one of their own laid down.

At the graveyard, mourners gathered 'round the grave where the preacher prayed and said to the other gang members, "To the friends of Sirlentay and anyone involved in gang activities or anything that ain't of God: Set aside your hurt, find God, and walk away from the thug life."

As the casket was lowered, Rich's mom wept hard and crumbled into the arms of her husband. Friends who gathered chanted, "Rich--- Rich--- Rich."

When all of the people stopped surrounding the mother with hugs and kisses, I stepped to her. "I'm sorry about your loss. You kno' I love you like my own mom. If you need me, let me kno', and I got you." I slipped her a rack in her hand.

She smiled. "You didn't have to do that, but thank you so much. I plan on seeing you for holidays when I make that sweet potato pie that you like."

I chuckled. "I'm not going to forget you." I shook her husband's hand and gave him a gangsta hug. He was cool. I gave Bridget a bear hug and told her to get at me if she needed anything, and I walked to the car.

One of Rich's homeboys named Steel walked over where I was. He gave me a dap and pound hug. "What it do?" he asked.

"It's all good on my end. Trippin' 'bout what happened to my boy," I told him.

He nodded. "We got our eyes and ears open to the streets, and we gon' have to get at whoever did the shit. My homey didn't deserve to go out like that," he said, shaking his head.

Our conversation was interrupted when a bunch of police showed up. Popo converged on some cars outside the cemetery, searching the people and the cars saying, "We're looking for weapons, and someone gave a description saying there was shooting earlier."

I got ghost and was in the wind. I had paid my respects, but I had a feeling that a war was 'bout to be set off 'cause Rich's boys wasn't gon' let that shit ride til they found out who smashed him.

The Disloyalty Showed Up

Sayveon

I made it to Pops' crib and rang the doorbell. He stepped to the door in his pajamas with bags under his eyes. He looked like he hadn't slept a wink all night. I figured that he must've been stressing over what went on with Rich and Jackie. I knew that Pops loved and cared about her a lot. I asked him, "Pops, you look like you ain't been sleepin'. You good?"

He walked to the patio and leaned over in his chair, coughing with a cigar in his hand. "Jackie's mother doesn't want me to attend her funeral. She thinks I may have had something to do with her murder, but I'm not worrying over that. I'm goin' to be just fine. What brings you over?" he wanted to know. He finally caught his breath and ran his hands through his stringy hair.

"I've been driving yo' whip fo' a minute, but now it's time for me to get my own. You still cool wit' yo' buddy that owns that Mercedes Benz place off of 55?" I asked and sat down in a chair at the table beside him.

"Yes, I can contact him right now. Tell me the color and model that you want, and he will hook you up today if he's in town."

"I want a nice whip --- prob'ly a black one, and I want the nicest one. I ain't trippin' the price just tell him to let me cop one ASAP," I bragged.

He nodded and changed the convo. "I see you're still dressed up. How did things go at the funeral?"

"It was straight. 'Bout as good as you can expect."

Pops sat straight up. "Son, I haven't always lived a luxurious life. I grew up in poverty, and my family struggled to make ends meet. When I was a small boy, I knew that I wanted to be amazing. We all want to be successful, happy, and regarded as important figures in our fields. I'm sure that you've heard of all the keys to success before: planning, hard work, perseverance, etc..."

I nodded. "Yes," I agreed.

He took a long drag off the cigar and blew thick smoke rings that rose above my head and floated across the room. He started again, "There is one factor that will make or break your success: The people you surround yourself with."

"True," I added.

"I brought myself up from rags to riches. At one time in my younger life, I lived from one penny paycheck to the next back in Cuba. I made up my mind that I was tired of living like that. I looked around at my friends and noticed that one of them, who wasn't particularly smart or talented, had become quite wealthy. I asked him how he accrued his wealth and how he was able to become so fortunate. The wealthy man's response was simple,

'Keep the right company.' I took that advice to heart, and you know what I did?"

I shook my head no, eating up the jewels that Pops was droppin'.

He looked directly in my eyes. "Son, I applied it. I noticed that all of my other friends hated hard work and had no desire to improve themselves. Therefore, I sought out new friends who had made something of themselves. After I had completely replaced the people in my circle, I decided to make a list. The list was simple. It had a column for people who would improve my life and an area for people who would drag me down. If someone could improve my life, I spent as much time as possible around them. If they would bring me down, I wasn't around for more than five minutes. After following my 'make' or 'break' list, I became a millionaire within three years."

For the first time in my life, I saw his eyes water. Pops cleared his throat and looked away. "I feel you, Pops," I said, understanding exactly what he was feeling.

I wondered where the conversation was going and if he knew that I had banged his daughter. I leaned back in the seat and observed his every movement.

His voice cracked when he said, "I don't want anyone around me who has betrayed me. Being betrayed by an associate is essentially the same feeling you have when you lose your best friend through illness, or in a tragic accident. I have experienced both, and both times my world was rocked. I felt as though an earthquake had hit, only the tremors didn't stop as soon." He glanced over at me. "Rich and Jackie betrayed me, and the punishment for betrayal is death. While you two were down in Florida, I found out what Jackie was doing. My people sent this to me." He browsed through his cell on the table and said, "Here, look at this."

I grabbed the phone. There was a picture of Rich and Jackie holding hands and going into a club. I kept scrolling and another picture showed Rich and Jackie sharing a French kiss inside of her car. The third picture was of Rich driving away from the club in her whip. "Damn," was all I said. It all came crashing down, and Rich got caught in the wrong.

Three hours later, I was leaving Pops' crib in my brand new Mercedes Benz C-Class that hit my pockets for sixty racks. Pops wasn't lying when he made it known that he had the hook up. His friend knocked two g's off the car and had someone to deliver it directly to Pops' crib for me. I left there thinking of how things had played out with Rich and Jackie. I would have never guessed that my boy was fuckin' Jackie behind Pops' back.

On the way home, my cell rang. I looked down and noticed it was a Florida number. I answered on the second ring.

"Yep. What's up?" I said.

"Hi, Sayveon. It's Jia. How are you doing?" she asked, sweetly.

"I'm Gucci. What's up wit' you, babygirl?"

"Not much. I thought about you and wanted to give you a call and say hi. I'm actually coming to Louisiana in a few weeks for my great-aunt's eightieth birthday party. I was wondering if we could meet up while I'm close by."

I hesitated and wondered what I had going on in the next few weeks that would prevent me from meeting up with her. "Yep, that'll be good. Come to Mississippi. I'll put you up in a room or you can chill at my crib if you want to spend the weekend or something, I'm down for that," I tossed at her.

"I would like that. I could stay at your place, but only if you can keep your hands to yourself," she teased and laughed behind her comment.

"I can't agree to that one." I chuckled.

We wrapped up the conversation and got off the phone. Ole' girl was feeling my swag all the way in Florida. Damn, I was a cold piece of work. My mack game was official, and all the hoes loved this shit.

A few seconds later, my phone was going off again. I picked it up from the seat and a smile came across my face when I saw the number.

"What's up baby?" I asked.

"Hey, daddy. What you doing?" my princess Janay, asked, sounding like a li'l angel.

"Driving. 'Bout to head to the crib. What's up wit' you?"

"Nothing. I miss you, daddy. I had a bad dream that my mama was crying 'cause a mean man shot her, and she kept calling my name," she whined.

It hurt that I had popped Peachy, but the bitch was foul for what she let go on with my shawdy. Trying to keep my daughter calm I said, "It's gon' be alright, li'l mama. Yo' daddy gon' take care of you and love you forever."

"Okay," she softly said. "I'll talk to you later."

"I love you, baby," I said to her.

"Love you, too."

We got off, and I really missed my li'l girl. I had been coming to the grandma's house visiting wit' her, but I hadn't had enough time to get her and let her spend the night with me. I loved my girls and regardless of how doggish I was in the streets, I'd kill for one of my daughters. I hoped to get better one day. I never wanted a man to treat one of them the way I had done their mothers. Reality had started to kick in, and I needed to make some changes 'cause mothafuckas was falling like flies 'round me. I just had to stay on top of my shit so that I wouldn't be next. I had somebody after me, and I still hadn't found out who the nigga was. In due time, he was bound to slip. When he did, I was sho' to be strapped and ready.

Late Night Freak

Sayveon

After I climbed in bed, a warm mouth kissed my eyes. It then moved down to my cheek, and a wet tongue circled my lips. She moved downward while kissing my neck, and I ran my fingers through her long blonde hair. She looked up at me, and we tongued each other down. Ginger's vanilla colored naked frame climbed on top and straddled me. She leaned down, slow grinded her pussy on my leg, and rubbed her hand up and down my bare chest. Leaning back, I felt her hand touch my boxers and pull 'em down enough for her hand to grab my pipe and stroke it up and down.

I put one of her nipples in my mouth and sucked on it, running my tongue around it. Ginger let out, "Mmm--- Sayveon, that feels so good, baby." I rolled her over on her back. I could tell she was horny by the way she laid there playin' in that pussy wit' her finger. She circled her clit and moaned, "I'm so wet, baby." I gapped her legs wide open, lowered my head to her inner thigh, and licked up and down. I heard her release a whimper and arched her hips. I figured that was her way of trying to test me to see if I'd eat her out. Nah, I wasn't rockin' that way. My bunny was a cool girl, but she wasn't my bitch. I wasn't 'bout to put my tongue on her kitty hole or her clit. I saved that kind of treatment for my main woman who played the wifey position.

I ran my tongue close to her slippery wet pussy, but didn't go there. I slid a finger up her tight hole, and she gasped. I added a second finger and curled 'em both upward, she shivered and bucked her hips. I knew that I had hit her spot. She started to cry out, "Oh God! Sayveon, I'm---about---to---cum, daddy." I felt her squeeze down on my fingers and soaked 'em up in a rush. She moved my hand from her insides. "I can't take anymore." She looked at me and smiled, "Your turn."

I reached over and switched the lamp light on by the bed. It made me rock hard to see a bitch pleasing me. Ginger pulled my boxers down and off. My dick sprung out, and the tip shined with pre-cum. She opened her mouth wide, and I could tell she was fiending to suck me off by the way she moaned as she licked and swirled her tongue around the head. Babygirl's head bobbed up and down while her hand went up and down my dick to the rhythm of her sloppy slurps. Her mouth moved to my balls as she sucked each one with perfection while still jerking me off. My dick throbbed. She directed her mouth back up and pushed me down as deep as she could. I sprayed cum down her throat. She held her neck back and swallowed. "Ooh, you taste so sweet and salty," she cooed. "Yummy, yummy, that's good for my tummy," she rhymed, rubbed her stomach, and let out a giggle.

I held my snow-bunny in my arms and sighed. "In 'bout two weeks, I'ma need you to make a drop in Memphis for me. Can you handle that?" I asked, rubbing up and down her arm.

She looked up at me. "Baby, I don't have a problem doing anything you ask." She grabbed my soft dick in her hand. "You make me feel so good. There's nothing I won't do for you." She cleared her throat. "Can I ask you a question, daddy?"

"Yep."

"I know there are no strings attached and we're just enjoying each others company. I need you to show me a little respect around your child's mother." She mumbled under her breath, "I hate that woman."

I had already spit some major game in her ear earlier before she came, but I was willing to rehearse some of my lines in order to keep her in my corner. She was bringing me the bread and making moves for me in the streets. I figured she deserved to hear some sweet talk in order to keep her on my team. I hesitated for a minute in order to say the right shit, but my talk was superb. I could kick game wit' confidence.

I lifted her head up with a finger and stared into her ocean blue eyes. "Don't trip that. Don't be buggin' out on my baby mom's coming over, that's nothing. Play yo' position and if you play it right you may end up being my bottom bitch. I mean, you got the credentials. Yo' body tight, you sexy, and you kno' how to make that money. So, don't worry 'bout nothing. I got you." I kissed her on her small nose.

She giggled. "I love the way you put that, but I don't know what a bottom bitch is. I want to be a top bitch."

I shook my head and played along. I was too tired to break down my slanguage. Dayum! "Aight, baby, you may just get yo' wish."

Ginger wasn't the brightest bulb, but she served her purpose and fattened my pockets pushin' weight and bringing me that dough. I fell asleep with her in my arms, and I knew that my bunny would be 'round for a long time.

Two Weeks Later

Sayveon

I met up with the Jia chick early one Friday morning at IHOP's on I-55 for breakfast. She wanted to stay til Sunday and then drive back out to Florida. We stepped into the restaurant and heads turned. A group of black chicks in a booth in front of me looked her up and down and then continued eating. She was looking jazzy in a pair of dark blue skinny jeans, a silver top, a black thin jacket, and silverish snakeskin stiletto boots. I got fresh and went for the casual look in a khaki and black plaid Armani shirt, black slacks, and a pair of casual khaki and black Burberry shoes. We were seated, and the waitress came over to the table. "Thank you for coming in to IHOPS. I'm Lawanda, and I'll be serving you this morning," the young, short, brown skinned girl said.

I browsed through the menu and placed my order. "I'll take the breakfast sampler and a glass of OJ."

Jia said, "And I'll take the same thing. Orange juice and all."

Lawanda nodded with a smile and walked to the kitchen area.

I broke the ice. "What's been up wit' you?"

"Not much. I've been doing the same old same old. I'm still managing one of the restaurants, hiring and firing, and trying to keep the customers happy.

My trip to Lousiana helped to relieve some stress, and I enjoyed not having to be under lots of pressure like I am at work. My aunt was soooo surprised by her birthday party. I loved being there, and I needed that family time," she explained. We talked back and forth before our food came back out. We grubbed, laughed, and talked. I liked her and I wanted to make sure she enjoyed herself while she was here.

Around seven o'clock that night, I invited Ginger over to have drinks with me and Jia. Two hours later, I had two dymed up chicks in the living room laughin' and feeling good off the Henny and Coke. Ginger and Jia both sat on the sofa. Ginger wore a black mini dress, black pumps, and smelled delicious. She flicked her hair and stared at Jia who was lounging in a pair of polka dot coochie cutters that showed that camel toe and a white spaghetti strapped tank top. I could see that her nipples had gotten hard, and I could see the small round circles through her tiny shirt. I got up and went into the kitchen. I said over my shoulder, "I'm 'bout to refill my cup. Dayum, the liquor got me feeling good."

"Me too," Ginger agreed.

I reached over on the countertop, grabbed the Henny, and poured it over a tall glass filled with ice cubes. I was lightly stirring my drink when Ginger came in and nibbled on my ear. "Daddy, I like that female that's in there. Think she'll agree to a threesome? I'm horny." She pressed her pussy against my crotch.

I smiled. Ginger was a hot li'l freak who was down for whatever, and I liked that 'bout her. "I don't even kno', Ma. Shid, try it and see," I encouraged full of that silly juice and feeling good. I took a sip from my glass and followed Ginger back up front.

Ginger plopped down next to Jia who was sippin' from her glass. Her eyes had turned slightly red, and she laughed a lot. I knew she was buzzing hard. Ginger looked at her. "I think you're hot. You're beautiful, and I'd love to taste your lips," she boldly flirted. The two stared directly into the others eyes. Ginger leaned over, and their lips touched. They began to slob each other down. My dick got hard as a brick off that shit and Ginger grabbed Jia by the hand and walked over to me and led us both into my room down the hall.

When we got to the room, the two women began to undress, clothes falling to the floor and climbed into bed. They silently gazed at each other for a few seconds and then reached out simultaneously and placed their hands on each others shoulder. I stood in the doorway and watched Ginger pull Jia closer. Ginger flashed a quick glance at me like she was waiting for me to give her reassurance. Her mouth opened and locked onto Jia's with her arms sliding 'round Jia's back.

The two chicks explored each others mouths and held on to one another tighter. Their eyes closed, and their bodies were tightly pressed together. Their hands roamed up and down the other one, 'specially over their wet splits. I could hear the slurpy sound coming from the juices flowing and being played with. My dick was on swoll and grew long as hell while I watched them aim to please.

Ginger put one of Jia's breast in her mouth and fondled, played with, and sucked the rubbery nipple. Jia's head went back, and she wrapped her hand around Ginger, and pulled her face harder with her eyes closed. She smiled from pure pleasure as she felt her tongue lapping around her nipple. Ginger spreaded Jia's legs open and slid her finger up her hole. Her finger slid in and out of the wetness making Jia cry out, "Oh, shit that feels so good, baby. Don't stop. Please don't stop." She bucked and jerked until she screamed out, "I'm about to fucking cum!" Her body moved faster, and she moaned before her orgasm was over.

I took off my clothes, pulled out the first drawer and pulled a rubber out. I unwrapped it and strapped up for some pussy. "Who want all of this?" I asked, standing their butt ass naked moving my dick up and down.

Gingers legs flew open, and she laid down on her back. She placed her arms 'round me and pulled me tight. Her hands slid between my legs, and she wrapped her slender fingers around my shaft and guided it to her pussy hole. Her eyes widened from pleasure as my tip steered into her slippery opening. I slid forward, pushing inside of it. I thrust into her slowly but firmly for a long time. I pushed in as deep as I could, hittin' the bottom. I felt her move under me, coming up to meet me with each stroke. The whole time, I looked straight into her eyes, her own gaze locked into mine like we were having a staring match while we fucked. Then I felt hands cupping and fondling my nuts. It was Jia. I speeded up, beating Ginger's pussy up wanting to bust off. "Daddy, I'm about to cream all over this big cock," Ginger said. Her eyes rolled back in her head, and she jerked and shuddered underneath me. After some more hard pounds and long strokes, I filled the rubber up.

"Oh God," Ginger let out as her orgasm subsided.

I rolled onto my back beside the females laying there panting and trembling. The two laid in one another's arms. Ginger was limp and breathless. Jia planted small kisses on her forehead and softly stroked her back from her shoulders to the base of her spine. I thought 'bout what just happened and smiled. I had two bad bitches laying in my bed, and we all got pleased. I went off to sleep with one bitch in each arm, I was feelin' myself fo' sho'.

The Slip Up

Sayveon

I heard knocking at the front door followed by the doorbell ringing. I dragged myself out of bed. Jia turned over to her side and laid there resting while Ginger let out a li'l moan and rolled over on her stomach and went back to sleep. I glanced down at the floor and found my boxers and put 'em on and went up front, sleepy as hell.

"Who is it?" I asked.

"Hi, it's your neighbor, Jack Reynolds, from across the street," the country accented voice stated.

I let out a loud yawn, stretched, and opened the door. "What's up wit' you, Jack?" I wanted to know wondering what the fuck he was doing up this goddamn early in the morning ringing my bell.

He smiled. "I'm sorry to wake you up, Say-vy-yon," he tried to pronounce. "Um, did I say it right?"

I rubbed my right eye. "It's cool. What's up?"

"You know I told you if I saw anything suspicious around here I'd tell you about it. Well, last night I was coming home from choir practice and noticed a black truck driving by your house slowly. He went up here to The McCraw's house." He pointed two houses down at some neighbor's place and continued on. "Then, he backed up out of their driveway and slowly went back by yours. I got behind him and got the tag number. I think you should have this. He handed me a piece of paper and walked off. "Be careful."

"I 'preciate that," I said and closed the door. This was exactly what I needed, and I planned to get right on top of it. I went back into the house and sent a text to Pops. He promised me that he'd get back to me within' an hour. He had his people all over it.

Ten minutes passed when Pops hit me back. I answered on the first ring.

"What it do?" I said into the receiver.

"Oh stop it. I'm your father not one of your gangster buddies," he kidded and chuckled. "I have what you need. I'll send it right now."

"That's what's up and 'preciate that old man. Good lookin' out," I thanked.

"No problem." He hung up and a text message soon came through.

The information and address that came through damn near knocked me off my feet. "What the fuck," I said in a low tone, trippin' off the shit.

Later That Night

A gush of chilly wind brushed against me and stood the hair on my arms straight up. I laid in the bushes in the quiet neighborhood and got ready for what I was 'bout to go down. I looked up when I heard a car zoom by. I put the ski-mask on and pulled the hoodie over my head so the dreads wouldn't show. I had to be cautious and couldn't slip 'cause a slip-up could have the po's on my trail, and I wasn't tryna to catch a body charge. In the past, I mostly had my boy Rich watching my back when beef brewed and we went out and made niggas bleed. Being out there alone was different because I always had my boy, Rich 'round when I needed back-up for shit like this. It was cool now. I had to handle my own, dolo. I quickly glanced up again when the front door of the victim's house shut. I ducked and quietly put the silencer on the glock and aimed, waiting for the perfect chance to catch him off guard. If that was him, I was about to put some 'rounds in his dome.

The darkness lightened when the porch light came on and brightly shined almost in the area where I hid. I heard footsteps coming near me. The dude held a tall red container in his hand. He walked to the front of the house in a dark colored shirt and slacks, pouring a liquid on the ground. He glanced up for a second before he went all around the house emptying out some kind of substance. When the fume hit my direction, I knew exactly what the mothafucka was doing, 'bout to set that bitch on fire.

I pointed the chrome directly to his head, pulled back on the trigger and fired two shots. He dropped to the ground and laid there on his back. I dashed into the house running past the bitch ass nigga that I blasted. The front room was empty, only the television played down low. I crept into the hall and noticed two doors had been opened. I leaned my head in, ski' masked up and there Nakia and LaShune sat side by side on the floor with black tape over their mouths and hands tied behind their backs. There was big puddles of gas all 'round where they were seated, and I could hear them both mumbling, "Mm…uh..mm…" trying to say something to me, but the thick black tape prevented that. I snatched the tape from both of their mouths.

"Who are you," Nakia asked. Are you working with my husband to kill us?" She was shaking and crying at the same time. I shook my head no. "Well, what are you doing here?"

I untied the both of them, turned, and dipped out of the room. I took off for my car parked up the street in a vacant spot and put the pedal to the floor. Being that I once had feelings for Nakia, I put the animosity that I had for her aside and let her and her sister live. That wasn't part of my make-up to do shit like that, but I knew that eventhough LaShune was a hoodrat Rich cared for her. I did that fo' my homey who stayed down for me no matter what.

Breaking News

Sparkle

While Ontavious played with Layla in his bedroom, I went into the kitchen to grab a soft drink out of the fridge. My baby had made me feel at home, and we even discussed the possibility of me moving in with him. Life was good on my end, and I had no complaints. Thinking about how sweet he had been lately put a smile across my face. I held the drink in my hand, walked back into the room where the ten o'clock news was on, and laid on Ontavious' chest.

A black news anchor reported, "I'm standing outside the home of Nakia Anderson where she and her sister have been living together. Nakia's husband who was a former soldier apparently set out to kill the both of them tonight. The victim's say that the husband of one of the sisters tied the both of them up and told them he planned to burn the house down. They say he went outside and never came back inside. A tall male came in the room wearing a ski mask. He untied them and saved their lives. Both victims say they went outside immediately to find help. Instead, they found the man who tried to kill them. He was dead. Investigators are now investigating the crime scene and plan to get to the bottom of this."

The camera operator showed a picture of Nakia's house and then focused it back to the newswoman who said, "I spoke to both victims earlier and this is what they had to say."

Nakia popped up on the screen. "I'm just thankful to God that whoever the man was that came into the home saved me and my sister. I'm pregnant, and I kept thinking about my unborn child. I don't know why my husband snapped out the way that he did, but I'm glad I'm still living and not in a morgue somewhere right now." She looked to be a few months pregnant. Her belly was slightly swollen. I shook my head in disgust 'cause Sayveon was possibly the daddy, and that was a mess. I was just happy that I didn't have to deal with that dumb shit.

The sister, LaShune, showed up next lookin' like she was a bonified hoe. She moved her hands while she talked and her neck rolled. "I don't kno' who the dude was that helped us, but I want him to kno' that I love him for that. Good lookin' out, bruh," she said right into the camera and then looked away. "That crazy fool could have killed us. I have too much going on in my life to die right now. That man tried to murder me and my sister, but I prayed, and God showed up right on time. God is good, baby."

"We've been recently told that the deceased man had been recently arrested. He was out on bond and awaiting trial for running a bomb-making operation. The material was stolen from a weapons depot at an army base. I'm Naomi Brandshaw reporting for News station 16 Live," the young reporter stated. The news went on, and a new topic was discussed.

I burst out laughing. "Tacky as hell," I said under my breath.

Ontavious laughed too and imitated LaShune by saying, "God is good, baby."

We both cracked up and all I kept thinking about was how blessed I was to have a man that loved me. I no longer had to deal with the bullshit and all the drama. As LaShune stated, Hmph, God is definitely good.

A Big Surprise

Sparkle

Shortly after the ten o'clock news had gone off my cell rang. I picked up and greeted the caller. "What's up, Mama V."

She cleared her throat. "Hi, honey. I hope I didn't wake you or disturb you," she said, sounding cheerful.

"No, you're good."

"I'm not sure if you know it or not, but me and my new man are having our engagement party tomorrow night. I would love for you to come. It will be at the Hilton off the Interstate, and it starts at six o'clock. I was wondering if you'd be able to show your face. Come dance and have a few drinks with me," she said, sounding excited.

"You know I'll be there. I'm so happy for the two of you. That's so sweet." I smiled because that woman deserved to be treated right and pleased. Pops' whorish behind should have been kicked in the ass and dismissed a long time ago, I thought to myself.

"Oh, I don't want to deter you from coming, but I want you to know that Sayveon is coming as well. But, don't let that stop you from showing up having a ball with me," she said.

Disappointed, I said dryly, "Okay. I'll be there."

She got tickled. "Sparkle Davis, you better not be fibbing me, girl."

I cracked a half smile and tried to cheer up. "We're going to have a good time. See you there."

We got off, and I couldn't help but feel some kind of way about Sayveon coming. What the hell, I'd ignore him and be there for Mama V and Mr. Travis. I wouldn't let one monkey stop a show.

What A Party

Sparkle

Saturday evening I drove into The Hilton. The parking lot was packed with cars, but I was able to find a park in the back of the building. I murdered the engine and got out of my whip, looking like a dymed up movie star in a one-shoulder cherry red mini dress and a pair of six-inch matching red stiletto ankle boots with a red bottom. My hair was pinned up in a neat and elegant bun and my diamond necklace, tennis bracelet, and earrings had me looking good and on point. As soon as my heels touched the concrete, my eyes looked up and down the frame of a tall handsome chocolate man wearing a black suit. Mister Anonymous had gotten out of his fresh black colored Benz and when he made eye contact, I looked off so fast I thought my head would spin.

"Goddamn, it's that bastard," I softly mumbled to myself. It was Sayveon, and he had the nerve to bring the white chick and some Chinese looking thang with him. OMG, the audacity of that cheating asshole. Ginger had on a tight fitted black mini dress and black pumps, and Ms. Chinagirl had on a fuchsia colored dress that stopped about two inches above the knee and silver lace up boots. His cocky and silly ass was still up to the same old games, but I wouldn't feed into the dumb ish.

Ignoring Sayveon and his groupies, I strutted into the building with my nose in the air. I had no plans of letting his foolishness and ignorance affect me. "Good evening, ma'am. Can I help you?" a white guy who worked there asked when I came through the sliding door.

I flicked the long bang that hung down my face and replied, "Sure. I'm looking for Veronica Rodriguez. She's having her engagement party here tonight."

He directed me down the hall and into a huge ballroom with at least one hundred guests already there. Each table had been decorated with pretty pink and white roses, white candles, champagne glasses, and a bottle of sparkling white wine. Rose pink and white helium balloons and a huge bouquet of flowers had been placed over where the engaged couple would be seated.

My eyes scanned the room, and I noticed a beautiful face. It was Mama V. She looked over at me and hurried to where I stood. She kissed my cheek and smiled. "Hello, daughter. How have you been?" she asked, followed by a warm hug. She looked gorgeous in her long white evening gown that hugged her frame, perfectly. The bun neatly pinned up in her hair looked really nice. She cheesed wearing some sexy red lipstick on her small lips. Mama V still had it goin' on.

"I'm good. I'm loving how everything is set up. It's really nice," I commented.

Mr. Travis walked over to me in a white tuxedo, he embraced me, too. "How's my li'l grandbaby?"

"She's doing good. She's growing so fast."

Mr. Travis went over to where Sayveon and his two hoes were and held a conversation. It surprised me that he had even shown up, knowing that Mr. Travis wasn't his biological dad and all. I whispered in Mama V's ear. "My boyfriend sends his love. He had to work late and wasn't able to make it." I looked up and saw the male whore looking my way. "I'm shocked that Sayveon even came."

She gave me a small nod. "Yes, they have talked their differences out, and William still considers him to be his son." Changing the subject she asked, "Can you believe that he brought those two tramps with him?"

I got tickled at Mama V gossiping on the low. "It wouldn't be him if he didn't act like a hoe." I glanced over again at Sayveon and caught him still staring at me. I looked away.

Mama V led me over to a table where her two male Cuban cousins sat. She introduced me to them and told me to have a seat. I got engaged in a conversation and ended up enjoying myself after all.

A slow tune by Freddie Jackson played titled, 'You Are My Lady.' The tall handsome cousin of Mama V's looked at me and asked, "Can I have this dance?"

I smiled and went over to the dance floor beside Mama V and Mr. Travis. It was so cute the way the two of them held each other and slowly moved to the music.

The candles provided us with a soft, flickering reflection. Diego slipped me into his arms. I enjoyed moving quietly in his arms while the tune of Freddie danced through the air. The wine that I had been sipping pulsated through my veins and allowed me to relax and have a good time. Of course, Sayveon had to act stupid. He walked over and stood right beside me slow dancing with Ginger. I felt like clocking him in the face, but I wouldn't give him the satisfaction of knowing he had aggravated me with his li'l skeezer grinding all up on him like a horny hooker.

I heard loud racket, and the music stopped. I broke away from Diego trying to see what the hell was going on. Boy, when I saw it, I could have been bought for a penny. Pops staggered over to a table where guests had been seated and tossed the champagne bottle to the floor. Pieces of glasses flew everywhere, and the older female at the table screamed, "Stop it!"

And when I really looked and noticed what he had on, I knew he had to be losing his mind to come in there wearing a old worn out pair of short white pants that stopped above his kneecap. The white t-shirt he had on had a big hole in the front and the slippers on his feet looked to be at least twenty years old from the dingy white color. He slowly moved over to where Mama V was. She stood there and hollered, "Get out of here, Al, immediately! You old fool. Don't you come barging in here crashing my party."

Pops raised his hand and slapped spit from Mama V's mouth. She held her face looking like she was in shock with her mouth hanging to the floor. Mama V's cousins Diego and Setho, took off to where Pops stood. The next thing I knew, Diego gave Pops a mean left hook that made him stumble backwards. Sayveon ran to Pops' defense and pushed the cousin away from him. "Man, let that shit go. Don't be hitting on him like that," Sayveon barked. Sayveon leaned over and helped the defenseless old man off the floor. Mr. Travis walked over and pushed Pops in the chest. Sayveon pushed him away too.

All I could hear coming from the mouths of the guests was gasping and a few people hopped up and stood by the wall to get away from the commotion.

Pops wasn't done yet. He grabbed a champagne bottle from another table and threw it into the wall. "Bitch, I gave you the best life you could have ever had, and this is the thanks I get?" He raised his arms out wide. "You're about to marry this jackass off of the money I worked hard to make while you sat at home on your ass."

Mama V placed her hand on her hip. "You're acting irrational and making yourself look like an ass."

"Fuck you." He pointed at Mama V with his speech slurred and then pointed it at Mr. Travis. "And, fuck you too. You invited our mutual friends to this bullshit, and that's how I heard about it. You're a disgrace."

Mama V shook her head. Pops crept over to the table a few steps away and knocked the huge chocolate cake with the words 'We're Engaged' on it to the floor. As Sayveon pulled him away trying to calm him down, Pops proceeded to curse between spastic coughs and gasps for air. "You're---nothing---but---a---cheap---whore," he let out right before he held on to the left side of his chest. His breathing slowed, and he collapsed to the floor.

A crowd of people circled him while one lady claiming to be a nurse raced to his aid. "Al, are you okay?" the older Cuban woman who apparently knew him, asked in a loud clear voice. There was no response. "I need someone to call 911," she yelled.

"I'll call them," Ginger volunteered with her cell in her hand. Then the bimbo asked, "What's the number?"

"Shut yo' dumb ass up," I ordered and dialed the paramedics from a wall phone set up in the room. I gave the woman on the other end all of the info she needed in order to send some help and hung up.

The woman assisting Pops checked his wrist for a pulse and then placed her ear to his mouth. She began to perform chest compressions in a fast rhythm.

Shortly afterward, she pinched his nose and breathed into his mouth trying to save him.

"Pops, come on man don't do this to me," Sayveon cried, kneeling on the floor right beside the body that wasn't responding. I stood there almost unable to believe what I had just witnessed. I guess pain can make a person do the unthinkable. Pops situation made me a firm believer that losing the one person you once loved could 'cause death. I always thought the smoking would kill him. Instead, it was Mama V. To Be Continued...

Books By Jennifer Luckett

Caught In The Middle

No Win Situation

Trifling

So Gone

A Dirty South Love By Ca$h with Jennifer Luckett

Email- lovewriting1@aol.com

Facebook- Author Jennifer

Made in the USA
Lexington, KY
05 April 2015